THE ADVENTURERS AND
THE CITY OF SECRETS

By Jemma Hatt

The Adventurers and the City of Secrets

Copyright © 2020 to Jemma Hatt

www.jemmahatt.com

Editing and Formatting by Amanda:

www.letsgetbooked.com

Cover Illustration by Andrew Smith:

www.andrewsmithartist.myportfolio.com

ISBN: 978-1-9993641-2-0

Elmside Publishing

Other Books in
The Adventurers Series

For Jeff

Table of Contents

Chapter 1
Detention

One of life's great mysteries is whether detention is a bigger punishment for the student or the teacher.

"Of course you had to get yourself in detention on the very last day of term," scolded Mr Rottin to the small boy in front of him. "I could be starting my Christmas holidays right now, but no, I'm spending my late afternoon with you." Mr Rottin looked as pleased as someone who had been sprayed in the face by a skunk.

"It is rotten luck, Mr Rottin," said Rufus Kexley, leaning back in his chair and staring up at the ceiling.

"As if I've never heard that one before… and luck has nothing to do with it. What are you in for this time?" Mr Rottin picked up a report from his desk and read it aloud.

"Rufus Kexley Detention Report: Using a creative writing lesson to write a poem about farts. Hijacking the school's tannoy speakers to read the above poem aloud. Impersonating a pirate—"

1

"Arrrrgh, me matey!" interrupted Rufus, jumping onto his chair and making farting sounds with his armpit.

"Sit down." Mr Rottin glared at Rufus then continued reading.

"Impersonating a pirate whilst reading the above poem to the entire school during lunch; pretending to be the star of a new reality TV show—"

"I call it *Keeping Up with the Kexleys.*"

"I call it a ridiculous way to get yourself in detention. There's more…"

"Exploding Daisy Duncely's science project—"

"Hey!" protested Rufus. "That was an accident."

"Daisy is in the year above with your cousin, you shouldn't have even been in the same classroom."

Rufus folded his arms and sighed.

"Flying three toy drones into the school corridors; marking the numbers one, two and four onto the sides of the drones, which led staff to spend two hours looking for a number 'three' drone, which did not exist—"

Rufus erupted into laughter at the memory, clutching his sides.

"This is not funny."

"Using music class to—"

2

Mr Rottin pushed the lengthy list of Rufus' misdeeds across the desk. "Oh enough of this, I'm bored already. Why did you do these things? And more to the point, why did you do them all on the last day of term when I'm stuck with detention duty?"

"It's entertainment," explained Rufus, "and entertainment is art. No artist should be punished for their work."

"*Art?*" spluttered Mr Rottin, scrunching his nose. "Where did you hear that nonsense? Look, Rufus, I know the other kids all enjoy a joke, but where are they now, eh? They're all at their homes, which is where I should be."

"At the other kids' homes?"

"Ye— no, of course not, at my home!" Mr Rottin's face was turning pink. "Nobody gets expelled in the first term of secondary school here at Swindlebrook, but you're heading that way in your second term if this behaviour continues."

"*Expelled?*" Rufus swallowed hard. "I can't get expelled! Auntie Sarah would send me back to my grandparents. They're getting on a bit now so they might send me to live in Hollywood with my mum! And she's a disaster. Mr Rottin, I can't get expelled!"

"Boo hoo," sneered Mr Rottin, wiping his eyes. "Tell someone who cares. All I know is that I will not waste any more of my after-school hours sitting here with you when I could be at home watching re-runs of *Columbo*. So, get your act together… or you're out."

An hour later, Rufus hung his head as he got into the back seat of his aunt's car. Barney, his cousin's Border collie, sensed his low spirits and showered him with licks.

"What a way to start the Christmas holidays," said Mrs Jacobs, furrowing her eyebrows as she steered the car out of the almost-empty school car park. "We need to have a serious talk about your behaviour, Rufus. You can't keep getting into trouble."

"I *know*," murmured Rufus. "No more pranks… at school anyway."

Lara turned and scowled at her cousin from the front passenger seat. "Or at home!"

"I would cancel our trip tomorrow if Tom wasn't already on the train from Cornwall," said Mrs Jacobs. "You don't really deserve to go to the awards lunch, Rufus."

"*Mum*," gasped Lara, open-mouthed. "But *I* still deserve to go."

"None of you should really be going," said Mrs Jacobs, shaking her head. "It's only been a couple of months since you all took off to Egypt without my knowledge and got yourselves into a very dangerous situation."

"We *did* find a massive loot of treasure though," said Rufus, rubbing his hands together.

"That doesn't make it right, Rufus! I must be mad, allowing the three of you back together."

"Four," corrected Lara. "Barney's coming tomorrow."

"Well Logan and Dee aren't here, so we haven't got a plane to take off anywhere," said Rufus, staring out of the window and daydreaming about the time when they arrived at the airport in the middle of the night to travel to Cairo.

"Where *is* Uncle Logan anyway?" asked Lara.

"He's in America with Dee, pitching for a new TV series with some executives. And I'm sticking around for this school holiday to keep an eye on you, so there will be no more adventures!"

Chapter 2
The Awards Lunch

Later that evening, Mrs Jacobs drove the car back to the station. Lara, Rufus and Barney waited by the ticket gate as the crowds of commuters hurried through.

"Mum was right you know," said Lara to her cousin. "You've got to stop getting into detention all the time, it's not worth it. You could get—"

"Expelled," Rufus gulped. "I know, I know. I'll be different after Christmas. New year, new me…" Rufus strutted along the station concourse as if he were on a modelling runway, flicking his sandy hair as he looked over his shoulder.

Lara sighed. Rufus made everything a joke all the time. As much as he annoyed her on a daily basis, she did not want to see him expelled from school and sent to live with his mother in Los Angeles.

Barney lifted his head and barked. At the back of the commuter crowd they spotted Tom, carrying a rucksack and dragging a case with broken wheels. His eyes lit up when he saw his friends and he rushed towards them.

"Hey guys!" he said, tugging his case through the barriers with one hand and rubbing Barney's head with the other.

"You made it!" cried Lara, pulling Barney back as he tried to jump on top of Tom's case to lick his face.

"Auntie Sarah's in a *right* mood," said Rufus. "If you hadn't been on the train already, she would have cancelled our trip tomorrow."

"My mum and dad are still annoyed with me about Egypt," said Tom with a blush. "This is the first time I've been anywhere in two months other than school; I've spent all the rest of my time working at the castle."

"But you spend all your spare time working at the castle anyway?" said Lara.

"Well, yeah." Tom shrugged his shoulders. "Mum and Dad didn't really know how to punish me, to be honest. They kept telling me to do chores after I'd already done them. Herb was excited about the whole thing and wanted to keep hearing the story over and over."

Mrs Jacobs greeted Tom as they climbed in the car and set off around the corner for home.

"What time have we got to be in London tomorrow, Mrs Jacobs?" asked Tom.

"The event starts with lunch at one o'clock," Mrs Jacobs replied. "It's not far from Charing Cross Station, so we'll get the train that goes just before midday."

***

The next day at half past twelve, Lara, Rufus, Tom, Barney and Mrs Jacobs were standing outside Charing Cross Station. Tom and Mrs Jacobs were looking at a map on Tom's phone, while Barney eagerly sniffed every person walking past them onto the crowded streets.

"We need to go up that way," said Tom, pointing towards Trafalgar Square. He stared into his phone as he walked forward, colliding with a girl.

"Sorry, sorry," he said, before recognising the ginger-haired girl in front of him. "Daisy!"

"Hey guys!" said Daisy, Lara's best friend from school who lived across the street. "What are you doing here?"

"We're going to the Egyptology lunch," said Lara. "I told you about it."

"Oooh." Daisy turned to her mother and nudged her in the ribs. "Can I go, Mum? Can I? Can I?"

Her mother's face reddened. "Daisy, how many times have I told you to stop inviting yourself to places? Sorry, Sarah."

"Mum," said Lara. "Haven't we got a spare place 'cos Logan can't come?"

"Logan can't come?" Daisy's chest slumped.

"Logan did have a place," said Mrs Jacobs, "but I'm sure Daisy and her mum have somewhere else they need to be."

"Oh, I don't," said Daisy, tugging at her mum's coat sleeve. "Mum, you can see Auntie Iris without me, right?"

"Does everyone in your family have flower names?" asked Rufus, tilting his head to one side.

"Everyone except Dad. I'm Daisy, my sis is Rose, Mum's Lily, Auntie's Iris and Dad's... Martin. So Mum, I can go with them, right?"

Lily Duncely looked at her daughter's expectant face. "Only if it's alright with Lara's mum."

"Of course," said Mrs Jacobs. "But we should hurry. Tom, do you know which way to go?"

"This way," said Tom, moving forward and making sure to look up to avoid bumping into anyone else.

"I'll text you later, Mum," said Daisy, linking arms with Lara as they followed Tom.

The group made their way past the busy square with its statues and tourists and turned down Whitehall, passing Westminster Abbey and the Houses of Parliament. They crossed the road where the streets became narrower.

"It says we're here," said Tom, looking from his phone up at a large old terraced building. "I guess this is it."

After they'd made their way inside, the receptionist directed them down the corridor, where a man in a suit offered glasses of orange juice on a silver tray. They each took a glass and entered a large banquet hall, adorned with round tables decorated with flowers.

Lunch was a lavish seven-course feast of small dishes presented one after the other.

"It's not as good as Mrs Burt's cooking," said Rufus to Tom, as he devoured the dainty and artistic dessert in one mouthful. "I'm still hungry."

An elderly man slowly walked on stage. "Ahem," he said into a microphone. "Thank you all for joining us here at the London Society of Egyptologists' annual luncheon. And I would like to issue a special thank you to The Adventurers for being here today."

"Whoop whoop," cried Rufus, standing up and pumping his fist in the air. Deathly silence filled the room and he slowly slithered back into his chair. Lara shook her head.

"Err, yes," continued the speaker on stage. "Before we begin the networking part of today's event, I would like to present this plaque to The Adventurers for their part in unearthing two significant Egyptian discoveries this year alone. Lara, Rufus, Tom and Barney, please come on stage."

The four walked on stage to faint applause from the audience. They each shook hands with the presenter, including Barney, who politely held up a paw.

"And I would like to give an honourable mention to Dee Okoye, Logan Jacobs, Karim Salib, Maye Salib and Aaliyah Khan, who assisted in the discovery but could not be here—"

The door burst open and a man charged through, tucking his shirt into his trousers as he rushed towards the stage.

"I'm here," he said, jumping up the steps and clutching the startled speaker's hand. "Logan Jacobs, pleased to meet you! Hi everyone!"

Barney flung himself on Logan in delight as the crowd erupted into loud applause. There were several murmurs of "*Logan's Jungle Trek*", the name of Logan's former television show. A couple of women came to the stage to take selfies with Logan in the background. He posed with both thumbs up and beamed with a wide grin.

"Why does he always arrive in such a mad panic?" said Lara to Tom and Rufus under her breath.

"Look at Daisy," whispered Tom. They turned back to their table to see Daisy fanning herself with a menu and staring up at the ceiling.

"Yuck," said Lara, frowning.

Logan turned towards them. "Did I miss lunch?"

"Yes!" they all cried.

"Darn."

"Ahem," coughed the speaker, in an attempt to regain control of the presentation. "We are honoured to have a small selection of treasures from the most recent discovery here with us today, on short-term loan from the Egyptian Museum."

As the man continued speaking, Lara looked out over the rest of the audience. Her eyes were drawn to the back of the room where she saw a lady in her sixties with short blonde hair. She was holding her left hand over her ear and appeared to be speaking softly.

She's wearing a wire, thought Lara to herself. The lady certainly did not look like a member of security staff, as she was dressed in a floral jacket and beige trousers. She looked up and met Lara's gaze, then stopped speaking and smiled in a manner that Lara thought looked fake.

"Now, enjoy yourselves and do explore the artefacts from the Temple of Akhmim on the Fourth Floor," concluded the speaker.

The audience softly clapped. Lara began to descend the stairs to walk closer to the lady at the back of the room when a man stepped into her path.

"Hello, Lara," he said, yanking her hand and shaking it enthusiastically. "My name's Humphrey, I'm an Egypt enthusiast, one could say. I was thrilled to read about your adventures in the newspaper. I was telling my mother just the other day that I was coming here to meet you all. Hello, Tom! Hello, Rufus! Hello, young Barney! Hello, hello, hello!" Humphrey continued to talk incessantly to the four, his head wobbling with animation, without giving them any opportunity either to respond or to walk away. Lara looked past the over-exuberant man to spot the woman at the back of the room removing the earpiece and slowly walking to the bar in high heels.

Rufus desperately searched the room for a method of escape. He noticed Logan was busy entertaining a group of fans and taking more selfies. Then he spotted his aunt standing with Daisy.

"Auntie Sarah!" he yelled, beckoning Mrs Jacobs across from their table. "Meet Humphrey! He'd just *love* to talk to you about your work at the university."

Before Mrs Jacobs could say anything, Humphrey snatched her hand and jumped into conversation. Rufus slipped away, followed by Tom, Lara, Daisy and Barney.

"She doesn't look happy," said Tom, looking over Lara's shoulder to see poor Mrs Jacobs well and truly trapped in conversation.

"I saw something a bit weird while we were on stage," said Lara. But before she could tell the others, a security guard burst into the room, his eyes wide in shock.

"There's been a robbery," he shouted, as everyone in the room stopped in their tracks. "The Egyptian treasure's gone!"

Chapter 3
The Thief

The room descended into disorder as several London Society of Egyptologists officials ran over to the security guard, while other members of the crowd gasped in horror. Lara's eyes darted over to the woman in the floral jacket at the bar, whose expression remained calm as she sipped her glass of champagne.

"*She* did this," snapped Lara.

"Let's go over there!" Daisy and Lara marched forward before Tom moved in front of them.

"Wait," he said. "You can't just accuse people of theft… who are you talking about, that woman at the bar?"

"She hasn't been out of the room this whole time," said Rufus.

Lara reddened with frustration. "But I saw her talking into an earpiece." She tapped at her own ear. "Now she's over there smirking."

"She's getting up," said Rufus, glancing over towards the bar. "Let's go out by the entrance and see what she does."

The five snuck out of the door and down the stairs. Police were coming towards them from the building's entrance. Several bystanders were stopped and questioned, but nobody thought to question four children and a dog.

Once on the pavement outside, they checked behind them. The woman in the floral jacket was exchanging greetings with a police officer.

"They all seem to know who she is," said Lara.

The woman shook hands with an officer and turned to leave.

Rufus pointed to a white transit van. "Quick, behind there."

They crossed the street and concealed themselves as the clip-clopping of high-heeled shoes emerged from the building.

"Sebastian," said a crisp voice into a mobile phone. "It's done."

The clip-clopping continued down the street. Lara, Rufus, Daisy, Tom and Barney followed, crouching low behind parked cars. The woman stopped at the corner. A large black Bentley pulled up alongside her. As she got in, Tom quickly lifted his phone to snap a picture of the number plate.

"We'd better get back," said Lara after the car disappeared. "Mum might have escaped Humphrey by now and could be looking for us."

Mrs Jacobs had not escaped Humphrey, but the reappearance of the children and Barney allowed her the opportunity to make her excuses.

"Where have you been?" she asked, striding across the room. "The security guard said nobody was to leave."

"The woman in the floral jacket left," said Lara.

"Frances Battenbridge," said Mrs Jacobs, folding her arms. "Trust her to think she's above the authorities."

"Who is she, Auntie Sarah?" asked Rufus.

"An art dealer. She owns one of the most exclusive – and overpriced, if you ask me – art galleries in London."

"How do you know her?" asked Daisy.

"She turns up at museum events sometimes. Although I don't know why; none of the artwork in her gallery is historical; they only sell modern art."

Logan approached the group alongside a police officer. Daisy moved behind Lara and looked in the other direction.

"I'm sorry to keep you all here," said the officer. "The team's checking CCTV footage then we'll need to take some details from all of you."

"Just don't leave me lumbered with Humphrey again please," said Mrs Jacobs after the policeman had walked away. "He doesn't stop talking."

"Noted," said Logan, looking over his shoulder to spot Humphrey eagerly talking to a couple who looked as if they would rather be having dental surgery than listening to him.

"How come you're back in London?" Rufus asked Logan. "We thought you were in America with Dee?"

Logan rubbed the back of his neck. "I was... we had a bunch of meetings lined up to pitch a new TV show, but Dee said I was getting in her way and saying the wrong things all the time. I don't know where she got that idea..."

Lara smirked. "Can't imagine..."

"...So, I thought I'd come back here since I had an invite to this lunch. Shame I missed the food though... do you think there's any left?" Logan wandered over to inspect the lunch tables, looking for leftovers. He found a tray half-filled with smoked salmon canapés and sloped off with them to the other side of the room to avoid Humphrey's approach.

Daisy shuffled closer to Lara. "Who's Dee?"

"His girlfriend."

"No!" Daisy's body shrank backwards as if she had been punched in the stomach.

"I know, it's disgusting isn't it," said Rufus, turning his nose up in the air. "Old people shouldn't be allowed to have relationships."

"He's not old," said Daisy. "He can't be more than… twenty years older than us."

Lara turned to her friend with raised eyebrows and Tom quickly jumped in.

"Is anyone hot in here? Let's get some water," he said, patting Barney's black, white and tan coat. "Barney's panting."

The policeman returned after half an hour and took Mrs Jacobs' address details.

"I'll be in touch if we have any more questions," said the officer.

"Did you interview Frances Battenbridge?" asked Lara. "She left pretty quickly."

The officer burst into laughter, wiping tears from his face. "Frances… Frances *Battenbridge*?" he repeated, between sniggers. "That lady has donated tens of thousands of pounds to the society, she's the last person who could be involved."

Lara opened her mouth to object but closed it after receiving a warning glance from her mother.

"I've got to go into the office to do some work," said Mrs Jacobs, glancing down at an email on her phone. "Do you all want to come with me?"

"I'll take the kids and Barney home," said Logan. "Take as much time as you need."

Mrs Jacobs paused and then grimaced. "I'm having a flashback to the last time I left the children with you."

"Oh, that was then, this is now," exclaimed Logan with a shrug. "And we don't have a plane this time. The kids will get bored at the office, they're better off at home."

"Rufus' teachers say he gets destructive when he's bored," said Lara.

"Hey!" said Rufus with his hands on his hips. "Stop reading my school reports."

"Yes... I suppose it is best not to bring you all to the office," said Mrs Jacobs with a shudder as she thought about Rufus being near the valuable and fragile artefacts in her office. "Alright, I'll see you later back at the house. Daisy, will you let your mum know what time you'll be back?"

"I'll text her," said Daisy quietly, still hiding at the back of the group behind Tom.

Mrs Jacobs left the building to catch a bus down the street towards her office.

"Right, which way is towards the station?" asked Logan as they stood on the pavement.

"You're not really thinking of going home?" said Rufus.

"I was... where else would we go?"

"To track down the stolen treasure!"

Chapter 4
On the Trail

"Track down the stolen treasure?" Logan wondered aloud. "How are we gonna do that?"

"Well…" said Tom, running his hand through his hair. "We've not got *loads* to go on."

"Frances Battenbridge," said Lara.

"You're obsessed with her," said Rufus.

Lara shot him a fierce stare. "I am not."

"You've not stopped going on about her since lunch."

"Well you haven't got any leads," said Lara.

"I have, I just don't keep shouting them out in front of everyone to give the game away."

"I think that lady was involved somehow," said Tom, who noticed Lara still glaring at her cousin. "But what did you find out, Rufus?"

"I heard a policeman telling Humphrey that there have been other robberies of old stuff this year."

"*Antiques*, not 'old stuff'," corrected Lara as she wrinkled her nose.

Rufus scrunched his face. "Stop acting like Mr Rottin!"

"I'll look it up on my phone," suggested Tom, who was eager to end the bickering. "The robbery's in the news already; it's come up on my home page."

Tom, Logan, Lara and Rufus glanced at the story on the webpage. Daisy leaned in to look, until she accidentally touched Logan's elbow. She searched for the story on her own phone as the others read on.

EGYPTIAN TREASURE STOLEN IN LONDON

Part of the trove of Egyptian treasure discovered by the group of children known as 'The Adventurers' in October has been stolen from a building in London. Police were called to Westminster after the loaned artefacts, valued at over ten million pounds, were removed from a locked display case. Scotland Yard is calling for witnesses and the search begins for the thieves.

The robbery comes amidst a spate of antiquity thefts in recent years, including ancient Chinese treasures stolen from the home of Lord and Lady Sotherington just two weeks ago at their annual charity Christmas fundraiser.

"Look up the charity fundraiser," said Lara. "Maybe there are pictures; we can see if Frances Battenbridge was there."

Tom searched on his phone and they pored over a number of images of celebrities and other people at the event, but Frances Battenbridge was nowhere to be seen.

"Maybe she just avoided the cameras," said Lara.

"I can't see any pictures of her," replied Logan, who had been searching on his own mobile phone. "When you type her name in there are just pictures of cakes…"

Rufus looked over at Logan's phone.

In between fits of giggles, he managed to explain the problem. "You typed 'Battenberg' instead of 'Battenbridge'. Give it here I'll have a go." Rufus snatched Logan's phone and began searching.

"I found a guest list," he called out. "Can't see Frances on here though…"

"Wait…" said Lara peering over her cousin's shoulder. "There is a Battenbridge… Sebastian!"

"Frances was on the phone to Sebastian when she walked out of the building. Here are some pictures of him…" said Tom, swiping through his phone. "He looks like her."

Lara scowled at the picture. "Same smug face."

"He's going to be in London tonight," yelled Rufus, waving Logan's phone in everyone's faces. "At five o'clock there's an event… it says he's going."

Barney threw his head back and howled.

"What's up with Barney?" asked Tom.

"He's bored," said Lara. "He hates it when we're all on phones. Sorry, Barney boy," she said, fondling the dog's ears.

"I'm getting a bit bored as well," complained Logan. "And I'm starving!"

"We've got to go to Churchill's War Rooms," said Rufus, getting up and marching along the street.

"Will they have any food there?" asked Logan as the others followed Rufus.

"Is that all you think about?" Lara replied.

"Not all… but it is important!"

"Oh, come on!"

Chapter 5
Churchill's War Rooms

The six stood outside a pair of glass doors on the street.

"Are you sure this is it?" asked Logan. "It doesn't look like there's anything behind those doors."

"The War Rooms are underground," said Tom. "Winston Churchill led Britain through World War Two from down there, away from the bombs."

Lara, Rufus, Daisy and Tom looked up at the calm blue December sky. It was hard to imagine planes zipping through the air blitzing the capital city with bombs in the 1940s, filling the streets with smoke and rubble.

They headed through the doors and down a set of steps to a man seated at a security desk.

"We're here for the event this evening," said Rufus.

"You can't bring a dog in here," exclaimed the man as he looked down at Barney. "There's no kids on the list either as far as I can tell… wait…" the security guard stared at Logan. "Are you that fella off the telly? Horace! Horace! Look who it is!"

A second security guard appeared and gaped open-mouthed.

"It's you," cried Horace. "I heard there were going to be a few celebrities showing up but thought they were pulling my leg. Come on through," he said, waving his arm.

The two men seemed to forget about Barney as the six followed Horace down the stairs. They entered an underground corridor.

"This is the cabinet room," said Horace, pointing through a glass window into a room lined with a table and leather chairs. "Britain's war efforts were all led from this very room. How about I give you a tour around the place before refreshments?"

"Refreshments?" repeated Logan, his eyes widening. "As in… food?"

Rufus and Logan's stomachs growled in unison.

"We'll join you there later," added Lara quickly. "We can look around by ourselves, thank you though."

Horace raised an eyebrow and was about to speak when his phone buzzed.

"I have to go back up to the front desk for a while," he said with a sigh, reading a message on his phone. "Logan, will you sign an autograph for me later on?"

"Sure," replied Logan, flashing his dazzling white teeth. Daisy's cheeks blushed pink as she stared up at him.

"Wait till my Marjorie hears about this," muttered the security guard to himself as he returned up the stairs.

"Let's find those refreshments," said Rufus, rubbing his hands together.

"Yes!" said Logan with a fist pump.

"No," hissed Lara through gritted teeth. "Are you guys forgetting we're not actually on the guest list for this event? We gatecrashed it to look for Sebastian."

"He's probably over by the refreshments," said Rufus. "Let's go."

"Hold on…" said Tom. "It's only five minutes to five… we're early. The other guests probably aren't here yet. Maybe we should wait somewhere until we see who turns up… if Sebastian arrives with Frances, she might recognise us from lunch."

"Let's split up," suggested Lara. "There's less chance she'll notice us if we're not—"

Lara was interrupted by the sound of footsteps.

"Quick!" whispered Tom. "There's people coming!"

Lara took Barney into a small room sign-posted as the Prime Minister's office, followed by Daisy. They crouched beneath a desk. Rufus, Logan and Tom ran ahead.

Footsteps came closer. The girls heard Horace guiding visitors to the reception area for drinks and snacks. Lara strained her ears trying to listen out for anyone saying the name 'Sebastian'.

Ten minutes passed and Barney shuffled around restlessly. He rolled onto his back and Lara rubbed his belly.

"Can we get up yet?" whispered Daisy as she tried to stop Barney's legs digging into her stomach. She was about to get up from the cramped space when the sound of footsteps returned.

"So how did it go?" asked a smooth voice.

"Entirely to plan," responded a lady that the girls instantly recognised to be Frances Battenbridge. "This is becoming *too* easy."

"Sister, what are you suggesting? A greater target?"

"The ultimate target. I think you know what I mean."

But I don't! Lara wanted to shout from the small office.

The Battenbridges moved further up the corridor and out of earshot.

Another ten minutes passed. Footsteps hammered down the corridor outside the office. Before Lara could stop him, Barney fled out into the corridor, his tail wagging.

"Lara, Daisy," whispered Rufus. "We've got to go! They've opened up a trapdoor into the ground and it's still open!"

Chapter 6
Going Deeper Underground

Lara and Daisy joined Rufus, Tom and Barney in the corridor and followed them back towards the exit. They stopped over a cloudy glass panel with steps below.

"This was closed up when we came in," said Tom as he lifted the glass panel away from the floor. "Then I heard Sebastian and Frances come up this way and they had a key to unlock it. They said someone else is going to lock it behind them later. You guys go first."

Lara, Rufus, Daisy and Barney descended the stairs into a grey-walled and floored corridor below. Tom replaced the glass behind them.

"Where's Logan?" whispered Daisy, looking behind them.

"He went further along than us," said Rufus. "We'll have to catch up with him later."

They crept along the dimly lit passageway. Lara put a hand on Barney's collar to warn him to keep quiet.

31

"It *stinks* down here," said Rufus, holding his nose.

"It smells like that time you broke my science experiment and all the chemicals spilled out," said Daisy, pulling her jumper over her nose. "Rancid!"

"I can't believe people lived down here," said Tom as they passed a pantry area and a large dirty sink. Tom was used to less-than-pristine living conditions; one winter Kexley Castle had so many leaks in the roof that every bucket had to be used to contain the rainfall. As Tom's dad fixed one leak, another two appeared, until all the bowls, pots and pans from the kitchen had to be placed under the drips. Tom had spent his days running around the leaks emptying containers of water. Even a leaky crumbling castle seemed infinitely more tolerable than the dark and smelly underground tunnels, with cables and pipes jutting out of the walls at every step.

"What if Frances and Sebastian come back this way?" asked Lara, looking around them. "There's nowhere we can hide." One doorway to their side had been bricked up.

"Maybe it will open up in a bit," replied Tom.

They continued on through the underground corridors. Barney, who was walking ahead of the group, suddenly stopped and pricked his ears. He charged down the corridor and stopped again, this time outside another doorway that had been bricked.

The others caught up with him and heard the sound that Barney had detected – voices behind the blocked entrance. The voices were muffled and distorted, but sounded like a man and a woman. Rufus, Daisy, Tom and Lara pressed their ears against the wall, desperate to catch a few words. Moments later, the voices grew louder, then stopped completely. Barney took a couple of steps back and whined. He tried to pull Lara's sleeve with his teeth.

"Barney, wait," hissed Lara, releasing her coat from Barney's grip. The four pushed their heads closer against the brick wall, straining to hear. In a second, the wall swung open, sending them flying towards the back of the corridor.

"Gaaaaahhhh!" they all yelled at once, at the same time as Frances Battenbridge stood in front of them, releasing a high-pitched scream of her own.

"What are you doing here?" she scorned once she had recovered slightly from the shock. Her face, which had appeared so calm at the Egyptology lunch, was streaked with anger. "This is no place for children! Or a mongrel," she added, scowling at Barney who stood barking at her.

Lara's face turned red. "He is a pure-bred Border collie! And even if he wasn't, there's nothing wrong with mongrels."

33

"Shut the brute up," ordered a man who stepped out into the corridor beside Frances, carrying an envelope. "Before I hurt him!"

Lara pulled Barney towards her. "You will *not* hurt my dog."

"I'm going to call the police," said Daisy, pulling her phone out of her pocket and trying to hide the screen that showed no signal.

"You, call the police?" Frances smirked. "You're trespassing. It's you who will be in trouble with the police."

"We're not trespassing," said Tom. "We were at an event upstairs touring the War Rooms and the trapdoor was unlocked so we came down here."

"These kids were at the Egyptologists' lunch earlier," said Frances to her brother. "They must have followed me here."

"What is the meaning of this, following my sister across London?" asked Sebastian.

"What's the meaning of you two scheming behind secret doors in the corridor?" said Rufus.

"Insufferable!" spat Frances.

"There's no harm done, is there?" said Tom, holding the palms of his hands out. "We'll leave you to... whatever it is you're doing... in secret..."

Daisy, Rufus, Tom and Lara slowly backed away down the corridor.

"Wait," said Frances. She lunged towards Lara, grabbing her wrist so roughly that Barney instantly jumped up to defend his best friend. His paws landed on the woman's chest as she toppled over, dragging Sebastian down with her in a domino effect. Shocked but unhurt, Frances flung her clutch bag towards Barney. She missed and instead struck the lightbulb above their heads, sending fragments of glass to the floor as the corridor was plunged into darkness.

"Run!" yelled Tom.

The five pelted up the corridor. They turned a couple of corners where the lights were working.

"We're going the wrong way!" gasped Lara as they continued sprinting. "This isn't the way back towards the museum. We're trapped!"

Chapter 7
The Escape

"We'll have to find another way out," panted Rufus between breaths. "We can't go back."

They continued down one corridor then another, jumping over the cables and pipes that criss-crossed the floor.

Tom looked over his shoulder. "I think we've lost them."

"I think we've lost ourselves," said Daisy, as they slowed their pace to catch their breath.

Rufus spun around. "We could hide somewhere till they've gone? Then go back up through the trapdoor?"

"They'll probably lock it when they leave," said Lara.

"The glass was quite solid..." considered Tom. "It would be hard to break from the inside... unless we get something to use, like one of these pipes..."

Daisy put her head in her hands. "That's if we find our way back! We must have taken about twenty turns to get here!"

"The air's horrible," said Rufus as he squinted at the walls covered in cables. Barney jumped up beside him. "Hey, there's running water behind here..."

"No!" cried Lara. "We don't know that it's clean. Barney, stop!"

Barney sat back down and whimpered. He did not like the smelly underground tunnel any more than the others did. He stretched his paws then got up to wander back down the corridor where they had come from.

"Not *that* way, Barney," said Lara, "they might be coming!"

Barney sped into a run.

"Come back!" called Lara, chasing after Barney around the corner until he stopped and stared up to the ceiling. Tom and Rufus followed behind.

Tom pulled down a collapsible set of steps from the ceiling. "How did we miss this?"

"Fresh air at last," said Daisy, tilting her head to the ceiling with her arms outstretched as she took deep breaths.

Lara ruffled Barney's fur. "Good boy!"

Rufus squeezed past them all and clambered up the steps. He pulled two bolts across and pushed with all the strength in his small body.

"Gaaaah! It's too heavy."

Tom and Lara climbed up behind him and pushed their hands against the trapdoor above.

"Budge over, Rufus," said Lara. "After three… one… two… three!"

The heavy trapdoor lifted, almost sending Rufus, Lara and Tom back down to the ground as they struggled to keep their balance. Rufus jumped up to take a look.

"*Ow*," grumbled Lara.

"There's a street out here," said Rufus, whose sandy blond head was now at foot level in a busy pedestrian street. A little terrier dog on a lead started licking his face in excitement.

"Woof," barked Barney from below, eager to meet Rufus' new friend.

"Do you need a hand?" said the teenage boy walking the terrier. He lifted Rufus out of the hole. "What were you doing in the drain?"

"Oh, I lost my car keys," said Rufus. "Thanks, mate!"

The boy raised an eyebrow then continued down the street with his dog.

"Hey!" yelled Daisy from the ground below. "Don't just leave us down here."

"And why did you say you lost your car keys?" asked Tom. "You're *eleven*!"

Rufus shrugged and helped Lara, Tom and Daisy out onto the street. Barney bounded out alongside them, delighted to return to the fresh air. The group attracted several strange looks from the crowds of people walking past.

"Sheesh, you'd think these people have never seen four kids and a dog climb out of a drain before," said Rufus, rolling his eyes. A couple of onlookers sniggered as they walked past.

Tom replaced the drain cover and looked around.

"Where are we?"

"Trafalgar Square," said Lara, pointing to one of the lion statues.

Tom's phone started to ping from his pocket.

"It's Logan," he said, before reading the messages.

"*Am I still meant to be hiding?*"

"*Where are you hiding?*"

"*I'm hungry*"

"I'm starting to get cramp in my left foot"

"I'm hungry and I have cramp"

"Don't you care?"

"Hello?"

"Oh no!" said Daisy, looking back at the drain cover. "We have to go back."

Rufus raised his palms and shook his hands. "I'm not going back down that tunnel. Go back for him yourself!"

"It's alright," said Tom, "I'm calling him."

Tom quickly dialled Logan's number and told him they were at Trafalgar Square.

"What?" gasped Logan through gritted teeth. "You guys left without me? I'm hiding on the floor, I'm starving, I've got cramp in my left foot and the right foot now, my hair's a total mess—"

"What a tragedy," mocked Lara, overhearing the phone conversation.

"I'm *desperate* to go to toilet…"

"Erm, we probably didn't need to know that," said Tom. "We're sorry, really, but there was a situation… come and meet us in Trafalgar Square and we'll tell you all about it."

"Okay… I'll come and meet you then we'll find somewhere to eat. But first I need to find a bog because I *really* need to—"

"Uh okay, see you in a bit," said Tom, clicking the call off before Logan could describe what he needed to do in the bathroom. He turned to see Lara and Rufus staring down at an envelope in Rufus' hand.

"Where did that come from?" he asked.

"I picked it up from the floor when the lights broke," said Rufus with a grin. "It's Sebastian's!"

Chapter 8
The Ring

"Shouldn't we wait for Logan to get here?" asked Tom. "He sounded a little hurt that we went off without him."

"Yeah, let's wait for—" started Daisy, before Lara's icy stare stopped her mid-sentence.

"We'll fill him in later," said Rufus, who was already tearing the envelope open.

"There's too many people here," said Lara, who felt as if the Battenbridge siblings were about to walk past and snatch the envelope at any moment. "We need to go somewhere quieter."

She looked into Trafalgar Square, which was crawling with tourists, commuters and pigeons. Her eyes fixed on the four stone lions. A couple taking a selfie stood under one. The other three were empty. "Up there."

The four ran over to the second-closest lion statue. They helped each other to climb up the stone pillar and

Barney leapt up behind them. They sat between the giant stone paws, shivering on the cold stone in the December air.

Rufus pulled a couple of sheets of paper from the envelope and stared down at a list on the first page.

"'Lord and Lady Sotherington Christmas gala'..." he read from the list of around thirty events. "'London Society of Egyptologists'... hey! This is a list of all their jobs. With dates."

Lara peered over his shoulder. "Does it say what their next target is?"

"I don't think so... the Egyptologists' lunch is the last one."

"What about Churchill's War Rooms?" asked Tom.

"Not on here... let me check the other sheet."

Rufus turned to the second sheet of paper which contained letters, numbers and arrows. The paper was headed with the words *The Ring*.

"The Ring..." said Rufus. "Do you reckon that's what their gang is called?"

"Maybe..." said Lara. "Or an expensive piece of jewellery they're after. What are all those letters and arrows?"

They stared at the sheet of paper. To the top left-hand side were the letters 'CWR' and the number one. A dotted line connected 'CWR1' to 'CXS2'. Another dotted line ran to numbers three, four and five but no further letters were written.

"Initials?" suggested Rufus.

"It could be…" replied Tom, tilting his head to one side. "CXS…"

Rufus slapped his hand on the ground. "Charles Xavier!"

"Oh yeah, because the X-Men are behind this," said Lara, smirking.

"XS… extra small?" said Daisy.

"It doesn't sound right…" said Lara, resting her chin on her hand. "Ah! I know the first one. 'CWR' – where have we just been?"

"In a smelly underground tunnel," said Rufus matter-of-factly.

"Crawling out of a drain," added Daisy.

"Churchill's War Rooms," said Lara with a smile. "So 'CXS' must be another place."

They all leant back against the lion's paws and tried to think of different places in London.

"X-ray… xylophone… execute…" muttered Rufus to himself.

"Stop it, you're putting me off," said Lara. "Execute begins with an 'e', anyway."

Barney lifted his head and barked excitedly. Logan was coming towards them.

"Hey guys," he said, standing below them on the ground. "Your mum phoned me, she's back home now. I said we did some sightseeing and are heading out for food. Which is true, right?"

"Erm, yeah," said Tom, who always felt slightly uncomfortable bending the truth.

"We are sightseeing. This is a sight," said Rufus, staring up at the lion above them. "And we're seeing it."

"Let's chat about the more important stuff," said Logan, furrowing his brow. "Where are we going to eat?"

Lara bent down and patted Barney. "The restaurants around here probably won't let him in."

"Oh," said Tom, his eyes widening. "There's a Christmas market at Leicester Square; they do food."

Rufus' eyes lit up. "I didn't know there was a Christmas market."

"Me neither," added Lara.

"Nor me," said Daisy, shifting her eyes away from Logan.

"Me neither…" said Logan, scratching his head. "Was I meant to?"

"Uh, no," said Tom, putting his hands in his pockets. "I read about it online… this website had a list of all the Christmassy stuff you could do in London. We don't get stuff like that in the village back home."

"They must do stuff for Christmas though?" asked Lara.

"Yeah… sort of. There's a ceremony every year where they turn on the Christmas tree lights on the village green. Last year one of the sets didn't work so only the bottom half of the tree was lit up. There's a Santa's Grotto too that I used to go to a few years ago… but Santa is always Toby from school's dad."

The six headed up the pavement. The centre of Leicester Square was filled with market stalls selling warm festive treats from bratwurst sausages with fried onions to churros drizzled in chocolate.

"I want one of everything," said Rufus, staring dreamily at a display of pizza slices.

"Me too," said Logan, pulling his wallet from his pocket. "You kids have got your own money, right?"

"I have some," said Tom, who had been saving his pocket money for two months for his trip to London.

Daisy took a fancy floral purse from her pocket. "I've got some too."

"What about you two?"

"No," said Rufus. "Cough up!"

Lara held out her palm. "You owe us money from before you went to America anyway."

Logan grunted and handed out cash to Lara.

"Fine. Get yourselves what you want, I'll be over by those giant hotdogs."

The others walked around the food market and bought different items to eat. Lara also purchased chicken for Barney and poured water into a dish for him.

"Let's go and get some of those churros," said Rufus.

They walked around the side of the market towards Logan when Tom put out a hand to stop his friends.

"That guy talking to Logan… it's Sebastian!"

Chapter 9
CXS

"Hide!" gasped Lara. They ducked down behind a stall selling warm mince pies.

"That smells amazing," said Rufus, lifting his head up to inhale the sweetly spiced goodness. Barney wagged his tail in excitement.

Lara waved her hand in front of her cousin's face. "Focus! What's Sebastian doing over there?"

Tom and Daisy peered around the corner of the stall.

"He's still talking to Logan..." said Tom, "now he's pointing down the street..."

"What's Logan doing?" Lara asked Tom.

"He's eating a hotdog and looks sort of, blank."

"Nothing new there then," quipped Rufus, rolling his eyes.

"That's good… I think," said Lara, looking up at the darkening sky. "Hopefully it means he's not telling him anything."

Seconds later, Sebastian moved on to talk to someone else. Logan finished his hotdog and looked around. He strode towards the stand where the five were hiding.

"Down here," called Tom.

Logan spun around.

"Don't look at us, pretend you're looking at the mince pies!" Lara pointed to the stall above their heads.

"And buy some for us while you're at it," pleaded Rufus.

"Hmm, they do smell good," said Logan, staring straight ahead as he pulled his wallet from his pocket. "Some guy just asked me if I've seen four kids and a dog – something about a mix-up and his papers were picked up."

"You didn't tell him it was us, did you?" asked Lara, covering her face with her hands.

Logan rolled his eyes. "You guys always underestimate me. Just like Dee."

Daisy folded her arms and shook her head.

"Logan, stop looking down at us!" Rufus said.

"No, I did *not* tell him it was you," continued Logan through gritted teeth, as he turned his head to the stallholder to hand over money. "I said I hadn't seen four kids and a dog. But this has your names written all over it, so what happened?"

"We'll tell you in a minute," said Lara, looking around. "We need to get out of here before Sebastian comes over!"

Logan stuffed the pack of mince pies in his pocket and the group hurried towards the exit. Tom looked over his shoulder but there was no sign of Sebastian.

"Do you think he knows the underground tunnel leads close to here?" he asked.

"Must do," said Rufus. "Where are we going?"

"The station," said Logan. "We've been gone ages; Sarah will be texting me again in a minute. Apparently this one is due back home as well." He nodded at Daisy who proceeded to lose concentration and walk straight into a bin.

"Woah!" she said, before quickly rejoining the others.

"But we still haven't worked out what 'CXS' is," said Rufus.

"Eh?"

"The papers Rufus took from Sebastian had a list of the places they've stolen from," explained Lara. "The second page had 'CWR' – Churchill's War Rooms, with arrows pointing to 'CXS'. We don't know what 'CXS' stands for."

Logan rubbed his chin as they crossed the road onto the Strand.

"I know you kids like working out all these crazy riddles… but you've got evidence now. Why not take it to the police?"

"Because that would be zero fun and adventure," answered Rufus, shaking his head.

"Not just that…" added Lara. "At the Egyptology lunch the policeman wasn't interested at all when I asked him to look into Frances Battenbridge. He just laughed it off."

"And if we took them these papers, it doesn't really prove anything," said Tom. "It's just a list of robberies that have already happened, it doesn't tell them where the goods are or who took them."

"X…" muttered Logan. "X-ray, X-Box, execute…"

"Not you as well," said Lara, clapping her hand on her forehead.

Outside the station she stopped and stared up at the building, a thought suddenly occurring to her.

"It's not the letter 'x'," she said. "It's a cross…"

Logan, Rufus, Daisy and Tom followed her gaze up to the sign for Charing Cross Station.

Chapter 10
Off Limits

"CXS... Charing Cross Station! How did we miss this?" asked Rufus, mainly to himself. "We were here earlier!"

"There must be some kind of underground tunnel here..." said Logan, his eyes wide.

"Well yeah, there is..." explained Lara slowly. "It's called the Tube..." she pointed to a sign for London Underground.

"I know that! I meant a secret tunnel. I'll get my phone—"

"Already on it," said Tom, scrolling the screen on his phone as Daisy looked over his shoulder. "Charing Cross Station had a Jubilee line service that was closed in 1999... the platforms and tunnels are still here but closed off to the public."

"That's got to be it," cried Rufus. "Let's go!"

"We're not just going to be able to walk into it," said Lara, folding her arms. "It must be locked if it's closed off."

"We can try…" said Tom. "I'm just trying to find where the entrance is."

Tom continued scrolling his phone. Rufus tapped his foot impatiently.

"Can't we just go and look for it?" he pleaded.

"The station's too big," said Lara. "That would take ages and how would we know if it's the entrance to the closed line or the entrance to a store cupboard?"

"Does it ever exhaust you being so *practical* all the time?" asked Rufus, as if being practical was a highly undesirable quality to have.

"Bakerloo line," said Tom, before Lara could answer. "There's a door to the closed tunnels from the Bakerloo passageway."

"Let's go, let's go!" Rufus ran a few steps forward then stopped. "Which way is it?"

"In the station and down the steps," said Lara.

The six hurried inside the station and turned down the steps towards the Bakerloo line. They shuffled in and out of the crowds of passengers carrying Christmas shopping bags, many of whom looked up in surprise at the Border collie racing along the passageway.

Lara used her travel pass to open the ticket barriers and hurried through with Barney. Tom, Rufus, Daisy and Logan followed the pair down the escalators. At the bottom they searched the sides of the tunnel.

"There!" yelled Rufus, pointing to a set of double doors with brown slats.

The group gathered in front of the doors. Rufus tried to open them. They were locked. Logan grabbed hold of the doors and shook them.

"Careful," said Lara, looking around. "People are staring at us."

"If you break in, we could get arrested," said Tom. "And we're on camera down here."

Logan let go. "You're right. We need someone to let us in. Let's go home and work it out."

They headed back towards the overground railway station. Rufus dragged his feet at the back of the group.

"We're giving the Battenbridges a chance to move anything that's hidden," he said.

Lara's face fell. Since Sebastian knew that they had the papers containing the 'CXS' reference, he already had a heads-up that they could find the hiding place or warn the police.

"Maybe we should warn the police and get them to open it up?" she suggested.

"They probably wouldn't," said Tom. "And what if they did and there's nothing there? Wasting police time is a crime."

They got onto a train towards Swindlebrook. Logan sent a message to Mrs Jacobs to let her know that they were on their way back home. Barney, tired from the day's excitement, lay on the floor of the train by Lara's feet.

"Can you find anything else about the Jubilee line section of the station?" Lara asked Tom, who was looking at his phone.

"I've been looking…" he replied. "They mainly use it for filming."

"Filming…" said Rufus, sitting up in his seat. "That's easy then… we need someone from the TV industry to get us in."

"Your mum?" asked Tom.

"Sheesh, not her." Rufus' mother, whilst trying to break into the film industry, had not been in contact with her son since her very brief visit to Cornwall in the summer.

"Who then?" said Lara.

"Dee!"

Chapter 11
Back to Swindlebrook

"That's *perfect*," said Lara. "Dee could help us out!"

"I'm not sure..." said Logan, staring out of the window.

"But she's a top TV production executive... and your girlfriend," said Rufus, scrunching his nose at the word 'girlfriend' as if he had been exposed to a very bad smell.

"I don't think we should force Logan to call Dee," said Daisy. It was the longest string of words she had ever uttered in Logan's presence, and she immediately regretted it as everyone's eyes turned towards her. Even Barney lifted his head up from Lara's feet. Daisy's face flushed scarlet as she fumbled her phone out of her backpack and pretended to read it.

"Well..." said Logan slowly, wringing his hands, "I'm not sure I can call her."

"Oh, don't tell me you've messed it all up already," said Lara, frowning. "You won't get anyone better, you know."

Daisy began choking and coughed into her phone. Tom handed her his water bottle and she took it gratefully.

"And more importantly, she can get us into the secret Charing Cross platforms," said Rufus.

"I haven't messed things up already," said Logan. "But she wasn't completely happy with me before I left LA…"

"Maybe give her a call?" said Tom, in a kinder voice than that of Lara and Rufus. "Tell her you're sorry about how things were left, and you want to make things right."

"Then ask her to get us into the secret station platforms," Rufus persisted.

"I don't know if it's going to work," said Logan, staring up at the ceiling. "But I'll give it a go."

Logan got up from his seat and walked towards the middle of the carriage where it opened out in front of the train doors. He took a deep breath and found Dee's number in his contacts list.

The others watched from their seats.

"He's definitely getting told off," said Rufus, with morbid interest. "He keeps trying to say something then getting shut down."

"He needs to let her express her feelings of frustration, then discuss altering the negative patterns of behaviour in the relationship," said Tom, repeating the relationship advice that he had heard once on a radio talk show.

Lara and Rufus looked at Tom in surprise, then looked at each other and shrugged.

"I think the relationship sounds doomed," said Daisy.

Lara sniggered. "You don't know anything about them!"

"Intuition," said Daisy, nodding firmly.

The train continued on towards Swindlebrook.

"We're getting off in a minute," said Lara. "Has he finished yet?"

The train slowed to a halt outside Swindlebrook Station. Logan returned to the seats as everyone gathered their belongings and exited the train.

"Do we need to get a cab?" asked Lara.

"My car's in the car park," said Logan. "I came back to your place first before I got the train up to the Egyptologists' lunch."

"So... is Dee going to get us into the secret platforms?" asked Rufus.

"Well... she said she'd think about it. I guess it depends... sometimes after we speak, she calms down a lot, other times she just gets angrier with me later."

They left the station and found Logan's battered Jeep in the almost-empty station car park. The vehicle coughed and spluttered as Logan drove back to the house.

"What are we going to say to your mum about all this?" asked Logan as they pulled up onto the driveway.

"We can just say we visited Churchill's War Rooms and the Christmas market," said Lara. "And leave the rest out. If she thinks there's any type of adventuring going on, we'll be grounded for the rest of the holidays."

"Well I won't be," said Logan. "I could carry on looking by myself."

"Who are you kidding?" said Rufus, wide-eyed. He was taken aback at the thoughts of the adventure continuing without him. "You couldn't solve this without us."

"Hmm, we'll say nothing about it to Sarah anyway," said Logan. "I don't want to make two people angry with me today."

Daisy returned home across the street as the rest of the group trudged into the house and faced a round of questioning in the kitchen from Mrs Jacobs.

"You went to Churchill's War Rooms?" Mrs Jacobs asked in a high-pitched tone. "With Barney?"

"The security staff got all star-struck when they saw Logan," said Lara, "so they let us through."

"Why did you want to go there anyway?"

"I'm studying World War Two at school," said Tom.

"Did you get the work done that you needed today, Auntie Sarah?" asked Rufus in an attempt to distract Mrs Jacobs' attention.

"Some of it," replied Mrs Jacobs. "But there's still quite a bit to do. I had hoped to be finished by now so we could all go out somewhere for the day tomorrow."

Lara picked up the kettle and filled it with water. "Oh, don't worry about us, Mum. You've been working so hard. I'll make you a cup of tea."

"Work comes first," added Rufus, nodding furiously.

Logan picked up the biscuit tin and handed it to Mrs Jacobs, before picking a handful out for himself. "Don't worry, I'll watch out for this lot."

"Right…" said Mrs Jacobs, looking round at the expectant faces in front of her. She wondered with a pang in her stomach whether the children were having more fun with Logan than they did with her. Perhaps she had been a little too serious about work over the past few weeks, she thought. "Okay, I'll go back to the office tomorrow," she said, whilst trying not to notice the look of relief in everyone's eyes. "But it would be nice to do something together before Tom goes back to Cornwall?"

"Oh, yes," cried everyone together.

"Okay, great… it's getting pretty late now; you should all get some rest. I'm going to catch the early train tomorrow but there's plenty of food in the cupboard so you can make yourselves breakfast in the morning."

Mrs Jacobs took a cup of tea from Lara and went upstairs to her bedroom. Tom, Lara and Rufus went to bed, each hoping that Dee would come through and find a way for them to get into the secret platforms at Charing Cross.

Chapter 12
Trainbusters

Lara awoke early the next morning and went downstairs to the kitchen where Tom and Rufus were eating cereal. She gave Barney his breakfast before preparing some toast for herself.

"Is Logan up?" she asked her cousin and Tom.

"Not seen him yet," answered Tom as he took his bowl to wash up in the sink.

"He needs to get up so we can see if Dee got back in touch," said Rufus. He marched upstairs and burst into Logan's bedroom.

"Rise and shine!" he yelled, shaking Logan's shoulders.

Logan grunted and rolled on his side.

Rufus leant close and shouted, "Logan! Wakey-wakey!" into his ear.

There was no response, so Rufus picked up the glass of water on the bedside cabinet and tipped it over Logan.

"Gaaah!" yelled Logan, sitting up with a start and wiping his face. "Rufus! Was that really necessary?"

"Yes! I couldn't wake you up. I need your phone to see if Dee responded."

"It's over there." Logan pointed to the windowsill before burying his face into the pillows. "I'll be down in a minute."

Rufus snatched the phone and slammed Logan's bedroom door behind him as he raced towards the kitchen.

"He hasn't got any messages," said Rufus, frowning at the phone.

"What about email?" asked Lara.

"Email... email... yes! There's an unread email from Dee Okoye." Rufus proceeded to read the email aloud.

"Logan,

"I've made arrangements for you and the kids to get into the Jubilee line platforms at Charing Cross Station. Go there today and tell the staff you're working on a new TV show called 'Train Trackers', exploring the history of Britain's railways. I've got clearance for you to be allowed in with a filming pass.

"As soon as you get some evidence of what these guys are doing you need to go to the police – don't try to solve it all yourselves. If there's any sign of danger you need to be prepared to walk away from this with the kids – we don't want another situation like Egypt.

"Stay safe and keep me posted, Dee."

Tom and Lara grinned at each other as Rufus read the letter.

"*Train Trackers*," repeated Rufus with a raised eyebrow after he had finished reading. "That makes us sound like a bunch of anoraks."

"What would you call our fake show?" asked Tom, raising an eyebrow.

"*Trainbusters.*"

"Because that's so much cooler," said Lara with a sigh.

Logan walked into the kitchen, still looking groggy.

"Dee got us filming clearance to go to the Jubilee line platforms," said Lara.

"What?" said Logan, rubbing his eyes before looking across the room at Rufus. "Hey, what are you doing with my phone?"

"You told me I could take it!"

"Did I? Oh. What else did Dee say?"

65

Rufus handed the phone back to Logan.

"See for yourself," he said. "And hurry up and get ready, we're leaving in ten minutes!"

The doorbell rang and Logan sloped off to answer it, followed by Barney.

"Hi," he said, as Barney leapt forward to greet their visitor.

"H-h-hi," said Daisy, stroking Barney with one hand and twirling locks of her auburn hair with the other.

"How's it going?" asked Logan.

Daisy's mouth opened and closed, a few times before she could stutter a few words.

"Thank... good... er... I mean... fine."

An uncomfortable few moments followed where neither spoke. Logan tilted his head to one side, while Daisy stared at the floor.

"Er, Lara, your friend's here," called Logan, turning behind him.

Lara came to the front door.

"Oh cool," she said, pulling her friend into the kitchen. "Your mum said you could hang out today? We're going to the station in a minute."

An hour later, Logan, Lara, Rufus, Tom, Daisy and Barney were talking to a member of staff at Charing Cross Station.

"What's the name of this TV show?" asked the lady.

"*Train Trackers*," said Logan.

"That's just a working title," Rufus interjected. "We're changing it to *Trainbusters*." Lara turned away and shook her head.

"Right... let me check."

The Transport for London representative took a phone from out of her pocket and spoke to a colleague for a couple of minutes.

"You're on the list alright," she said after putting her phone away. "But it doesn't say anything about bringing a dog?"

"He's the star of the show," said Lara, rubbing Barney's head. "We need to take him down the tunnels to make sure it doesn't spook him when we start filming."

"Alright, come on," she said, waving them on. "I'm Sally, by the way."

The group introduced themselves and were led down the steps into the Tube concourse and through the ticket barriers into the passenger walkway towards the Bakerloo line. They stopped outside the same set of double doors that they had seen the day before. Sally pulled a set of keys from her pocket.

The group walked into a dark space.

"Have to keep this place very secure," Sally explained as she locked the doors behind them. "For some reason people are obsessed with trying to get into places that are out of bounds. Only yesterday we had a report of some guy trying to force the doors open last night in front of his kids."

"Terrible what some people will do," said Rufus, shaking his head solemnly.

Logan's cheeks reddened. Thankfully, it was dark, and no one noticed.

"It is indeed. Now, where's the light switch…"

Sally fumbled around feeling the side of the wall using the light from her phone. At last she found a switch and pressed it. Bright lights from above revealed that the group were standing at the top of a large and chillingly empty passenger concourse area.

"This is so cool," gasped Rufus as he stared down the escalators that were at a standstill.

Lara felt goosebumps prickle her arms as she took in the familiar yet abandoned surroundings. It was spooky seeing somewhere so empty, that was usually filled with people. She wondered if this was what it felt like for the caretaker at Swindlebrook Secondary School when he unlocked the doors in the morning and switched all the lights on.

"Lots of filming has happened down here," said Sally, who was glowing with pride. "Come down the stairs, they're easier to climb than the escalators when they're switched off."

The group descended the stairs that passed down the middle of two escalators. Sally pointed out several facts about the area of the station.

"Sometimes the film crews like to bring their own posters," she explained. "Will you be bringing your own?"

"Err, no, these will do," said Logan, looking at posters that looked outdated.

"The last film was set in the nineties, so all the posters are from then. This way to the tunnels," said Sally, turning right at the bottom of the stairway.

"Where do the tunnels go to?" Lara asked Sally.

"This section goes under Trafalgar Square and connects up with the Jubilee line."

Lara shot a look across to Tom. Recognition sparked in his eyes.

"We can get the trains into the platform during filming, to make it look like it's still operational."

Rufus slid over towards Lara, Daisy, Tom and Barney.

"We've got to get away from Sally so we can look around properly," he whispered.

"How?" asked Tom.

"Distraction," said Rufus, before loudly clearing his throat. "Sally, did you know Logan was the star of his own TV show, *Logan's Jungle Trek*?"

Daisy smiled to herself as Sally turned to Logan, her mouth gaping.

"I thought you looked familiar!" she cried. "I loved that show. I used to watch that with my sister. Are they bringing it back?"

"Not at the moment," said Logan with a flick of his hair. "But there's plenty of opportunities coming up."

"Like *Trainbusters*," said Rufus with a wide grin.

"This is fantastic," Sally enthused, while unable to take her eyes off Logan. "All that time off the telly then you're back with *Trainbusters*, right here in Charing Cross Station!"

"Ahem," coughed Logan. "Yes… it's a thrill alright."

"What's it like to visit some of those remote places? Did you ever feel like you were in danger?"

Logan responded with a winning smile and started to tell Sally some of his favourite stories of near-misses with poisonous frogs. Sally giggled and blushed in response.

"Now's our chance," whispered Rufus.

Chapter 13
Exploring

Rufus tiptoed out of the platform, followed by Lara, Daisy, Tom and Barney. They crossed the large concourse area over to the second Jubilee line platform. Tom walked over to the edge and stared into the tunnel where it curved round into the darkness.

"Were you thinking what I was thinking?" Lara asked Tom.

"Yeah... one of those tunnels leading out from the War Rooms must connect up to these tracks."

"From here they could take the stolen goods up to the main station," said Rufus, "then get it on a train."

Lara shook her head. "The main station is covered all over by CCTV, they'd never get it all out that way."

"Sounds like a mystery for the *Trainbusters* to solve," said Rufus, rubbing his hands together.

"Urgh," groaned Lara. "Stop trying to make *Trainbusters* a thing."

A scrambling sound on the train tracks interrupted their bickering. Barney's ears pricked up, and in a second, he launched himself onto the tracks.

"Barney!" cried Lara.

The three looked across to where the dog was scraping a section of the ground with his paws.

"Barney!" yelled Lara. "Get out, now!"

Barney looked up at Lara. He wanted to carry on digging but his best friend looked angry with him. He leapt up onto the platform and flung himself at Lara, furiously licking her arms and legs.

"What was he after?" asked Rufus.

"Mice," said Tom, pointing to a spot further up the tracks. "I can see a couple more up there."

"Barney, don't you dare run off after those mice again," said Lara in a wavering voice. "We've spoken about this. You're not allowed to chase any other animals. Or jump onto train tracks. You could have been electrocuted!" Lara bent down and hugged him.

Barney licked her face and yawned. He loved Lara but certainly did not love all her rules.

"They're so cute," said Daisy, placing both hands on her chest. "Look at that one, scampering about. Look at his cute little paws!"

"Really?" Rufus raised an eyebrow as he mentally crossed out the idea of performing his fake mouse prank on Daisy.

"Daisy has some funny ideas about things that are cute," said Lara with a snort.

"The electricity for these lines has been switched off," said Tom. "Good job too since Barney was touching the rails with his paws just now."

"Can you see any letters or symbols?" asked Rufus, looking around the empty platform.

"Only on the posters…" said Tom. "And Sally said they get changed a lot for others so I don't think there would be anything hidden there."

"Where could stuff be hidden down here?" said Lara.

Rufus pointed down to the train tracks.

"Eww, gross," said Lara, pulling a face. "We have to go down there with the mice?"

"Woof," Barney answered, wagging his tail.

"They won't harm us," added Daisy.

"It's the only place around here they could hide anything," said Tom. "Where's Logan and Sally?"

Rufus darted back to the concourse and returned thirty seconds later.

"Logan's showing her pictures from *Jungle Trek* on his phone," he reported back. "That should give us an hour, at least."

Lara took a deep breath and gingerly climbed down onto the tracks, followed eagerly by Barney. She took a small LED torch from her pocket and pointed it down the train tunnel.

"I thought you didn't want to go down there?" said Tom.

"I don't... but we might as well get on with it. Come on!"

Daisy, Rufus and Tom climbed down from the platform and shone their torches after Lara and Barney. They followed the track around the winding corner where it opened into a wider space.

"We should spread out so we can check the walls and tracks for any markings," said Lara.

They continued travelling down the tunnel, Lara and Barney to the right, Tom and Daisy to the left and Rufus down the middle.

"Over here," called Daisy. She turned the handle of a door and it swung open.

The others followed Daisy and Tom into a dark tunnel and up some steps. The tunnel weaved around two corners, eventually leading to another door. Tom opened it and stepped onto a metal grill with light shining from below.

"Look," he gasped, pointing beneath him. "There's people down there!"

They stepped forward. Beneath them were the tops of passengers' heads as the figures stood and walked around on a brightly lit station platform.

"But the Jubilee line was closed at Charing Cross," said Rufus, gaping.

"It's the Northern line," said Lara, tilting her head at an angle to look down the platform. I can see a list of stops over there... we're still at Charing Cross but we've come over to the other side of the station."

At that moment, a gust of wind blew through the grill that the five were standing on. Barney hopped about, staring through slits in the metal as the air rushed through his fur.

"It's a train!" yelled Daisy above the sound of the rumbling and swooshing air.

Lara, Rufus, Daisy and Tom held onto the wall as a train appeared under their feet. The doors opened and crowds of people got off the train before others got on, all unaware of the five watching them from above. Soon the platform emptied, and a series of beeps preceded the train doors slamming shut. The carriages disappeared, sending another great gust of wind through the space above the platform.

"We're standing in the air vent," said Tom, smiling at his friends. "This tunnel gets air from the street down to the platform."

"So somewhere this goes above ground…" said Rufus. "Maybe the Battenbridges use one of these air tunnels to sneak their stolen goods around?"

"Would they use these tunnels over a busy platform?" asked Lara. "The Jubilee line must have these air tunnels as well and they'd be completely abandoned."

"We need to find them," said Rufus, leaving the metal grill just as another train thundered into the station below. "Come on!"

Chapter 14
Above Ground

The five retraced their steps through the tunnel into the room with the metal staircase and back onto the tracks of the abandoned Jubilee line branch of Charing Cross Station.

Continuing along the tracks, they turned a corner and came to a dead end. The train tunnel was blocked by a brick wall. Lara found a door to the side of the wall.

"There's another air vent tunnel up here," she called out.

"Wait…" yelled Rufus, shining his torch on the wall on markings carved with a knife.

Daisy squinted her eyes. "Three… 'LTM'."

"That's got to be the next clue in the sequence," said Lara. "After Churchill's War Rooms and Charing Cross Station. I wonder if it's up here."

They headed up another winding metal staircase.

"LTM…LTM…" muttered Rufus.

"London… something… market?" suggested Tom.

"I can see light," said Lara.

The staircase ended a few feet before the top of the air vent and was replaced by a ladder against the wall. A metal grate covered the opening with slats revealing daylight shining through.

Tom climbed up the ladder first, clicking a latch to release the metal cover. He slid it to the side above the opening and made his way back down the steps.

"Should we try to lift Barney out first?"

Before anyone could answer, Barney flung himself against the ladder and scrambled to the top with his paws and feet.

"Amazing," said Tom, his eyes fixed on the Border collie. "He's like a cat!"

"Go, Barney; go, Barney!" cheered Daisy, jumping up and down.

"He's climbing all over the place at the moment," said Lara, smiling. "Last week Mum found him sitting on the roof."

Tom stared at her. "How did he get on the roof?"

"Someone encouraged him," said Lara. They turned to Rufus.

"What?" Rufus replied. "I just think it's a good skill to have… and he can help me with some pranks."

Barney hauled himself over the top of the ladder, pleased with his efforts and relieved to be back in the December daylight. He woofed back at his friends in satisfaction.

"You will not use my dog to help you with pranks," said Lara, folding her arms.

"Why not?" asked Rufus. "We use him to help us find treasure and fight crime!"

"We do not use him," Lara protested, her face turning pink. "He is a valued member of the team."

"And he's up on the streets of London on his own," said Tom, nodding towards the ladder. "Come on."

Back on the street they looked around, taking in their surroundings. They found themselves in a narrow side street with brick buildings on either side.

Tom replaced the metal grate over the air vent tunnel and followed Lara, Rufus and Barney as they stepped forward.

"It's Covent Garden," he said, spinning round as he took in his surroundings. "There's the market." They gazed at the building in front of them with people bustling in and out with shopping bags.

"Have you been here before?" Lara asked Tom.

"No…" said Tom. "I like looking up places sometimes though, on my phone maps and pictures."

"LTM… London… something… market…" said Rufus.

Tom's phone rang and he pulled it from his pocket.

"Hi Logan…" he said quietly.

"I forgot he was with us," giggled Rufus.

"Tom… where are you guys?" said Logan. "I've tried to call you five times!"

"Sorry… no reception underground. We're at Covent Garden, in front of the market."

"Why did you leave? I thought we were going to search through the tunnels?"

"We did…" said Tom.

"Without me? Well that's just *great* isn't it… I come all the way back from Los Angeles to spend Christmas with you guys and you keep going off exploring tunnels without me."

"Dry your eyes, mate!" yelled Rufus.

"What was that?"

"Nothing," said Tom, stepping away from Rufus. "The tunnels had a marking on the wall… 'LTM' – come over to the market and we can figure it out."

"Alright, I'll make my way over there. Don't discover anything else without me."

"Too late for that," said Lara, looking over her shoulder. Tom and Rufus turned around. Opposite Covent Garden stood the London Transport Museum.

"What's Lara saying?" asked Logan through the phone.

"We've just discovered what 'LTM' stands for."

"*Seriously*? I'll be there in five. Don't go anywhere."

Tom ended the call and turned towards his friends.

"I think we should go in there," said Rufus.

"It's not free," said Lara, pointing to a sign with admissions charges. "And they might not let us go in with Barney."

Rufus sighed and placed his hands on his hips.

"Where's Daisy?" asked Tom.

They searched through the crowds and spotted a street musician playing festive songs on a trumpet. Two other performers walked around covered head to toe in gold paint. Daisy was chatting to an elderly pair of tourists, waving her arms as she emphasised her points.

"She's always like this," said Lara. "Every school trip, meal out, whatever – she chats away to everyone."

"Everyone except Logan," said Rufus with a giggle.

A large man bustled towards them.

"Oh no," gasped Rufus, slapping his hand against his forehead.

Lara followed her cousin's glance.

"*No!*" she echoed. "Can't we try to get away?"

"Who is it?" asked Tom. "Not the Battenbridges?"

Rufus shook his head. "Worse."

"Hello, hello, hello!" boomed Humphrey, wobbling his chin as he grabbed each of their hands. He held out an arm to grab Barney's paw who promptly hid behind Lara's legs. "Delighted we meet again!"

Chapter 15
Humphrey's Surprise

"Hi Humphrey," said Tom, breaking the silence as neither Lara nor Rufus had said a word to the enthusiastic man.

"What brings you all to the London Transport Museum?"

Rufus stepped forward. "What brings *you* here?"

"I work here!" cried Humphrey, unabashed by Rufus' rude tone. "Are you all coming inside? We could get some pictures of you all for our museum newsletter. We could call it 'The Adventurers on the Buses'!"

"We're just waiting for my uncle, although," Lara cleared her throat, "do you think we'd be able to bring Barney inside with us? I can't leave him out here."

"Hmm… we're only meant to allow guide dogs," said Humphrey, staring at Barney with his hands on his hips. "But I'm sure we can make an exception for the famous Barney!"

"Here comes Logan," said Rufus, pointing to a man running through the streets towards them. As Logan spotted the group, he tripped over a street performer's guitar case, sending coins hurtling across the street. Hurriedly, he scooped them back up as the singer shouted at him through the microphone.

"Sorry!" he apologised, returning the coins with an extra note from his pocket into the guitar case.

"That's a McDonald's receipt!" yelled the musician.

"Sorry!" Logan fumbled through his pocket and replaced the receipt with a bank note.

"That's an American dollar!"

Logan waved his arm in apology and made his way over to his niece and her friends.

"Humphrey is going to let us look around the London Transport Museum," explained Lara, slowly emphasising each word.

"London Transport Museum..." repeated Logan, "LTM... London Transport... oh! Right!"

Lara turned away from Humphrey and rolled her eyes.

"Come this way, I'll let you in through the back," said Humphrey. He led them to the back of the building. "Wait here a second, I just need to speak to my boss."

Daisy rejoined the group and a couple of minutes later, Humphrey returned.

"Sorry, chaps, the boss said I can't let a dog in until the other visitors have left. But we're closing early at two o'clock today, come back then?"

Logan looked at the time on his phone.

"Quarter to one... okay let's get some lunch and come back."

"See you later, Humph," said Rufus.

The six walked into Covent Garden market. They found a cafe that accepted dogs and sat down at a table.

"What can I get you?" asked the waiter, opening his notepad.

"A jacket potato and salad, please," said Lara. "And some chicken on a side plate, for Bar— um, for me."

"Quiche and salad for me, please," added Tom.

"A halloumi wrap, please," said Daisy.

"Hmm..." said Rufus, flicking through the menu. "A cheeseburger, please, with cheesy fries, mac and cheese and cheesy potato skins on the side. Oh, and some cheesecake, please."

The waiter, seemingly unfazed by Rufus' order, asked, "Would you like the cheesecake after the rest of your meal, or at the same time?"

"At the same time, please."

Lara scoffed. "*Really*?"

"Yeah… I might want something else for dessert," said Rufus.

"Something without cheese in I hope!" Lara replied.

Logan asked for the same as Rufus and the waiter went back to the kitchen.

Rufus and Logan entered into a lively discussion about the advantages and disadvantages of different types of cheese, while Tom stared at the table with furrowed eyebrows.

"What's up?" asked Lara.

"It's kind of weird that we've seen Humphrey in two places in two days," said Tom. "in a city as big as London."

Lara considered for a moment. Humphrey had made a beeline for them during both of their meetings, bounding over to them with gusto.

"He's just a nerd," she said. "I mean, he works at a museum and goes to historical society lunches in his spare time."

"Maybe," said Tom quietly, turning his gaze out of the window.

"Stilton is the smelliest," Rufus told Logan, rubbing his hands together. "Me and Callum hid a load of it in the history classroom, it took Rottin two months to find it."

"That must have *reeked*," gasped Logan.

"Like smelly feet after walking through a field of cow dung."

Lara scrunched her nose at the memory. "We all had to suffer for that prank, Rufus!"

The food arrived and everyone tucked in except for Daisy, who stared at her halloumi wrap.

"Aren't you eating that?" asked Rufus, slapping his chops. "I'll have it if you don't want it?"

"Um, well, er," said Daisy, shuffling in her seat.

"Daisy, come with me outside for a bit," said Lara, grabbing Barney's collar and her friend's arm. "I think Barney needs to go outside."

The three walked out of the front of the restaurant.

"This isn't good, Daisy," said Lara, putting her hand around her friend's shoulder. "You're barely talking and you're not eating... Logan's just a doofus really, not worth getting all soppy over."

"I can't help it." Daisy stared at the ground. "I just kind of freeze up! It's soooo embarrassing."

Tom stepped out of the restaurant and wordlessly handed his phone to Lara with a wink, before returning back inside.

Lara stared down at the screen.

"Yes! This is perfect. Watch this," she said, handing the phone to her friend.

Daisy pressed play and watched a montage of bloopers from the TV show *Logan's Jungle Trek*. Footage played of Logan falling, spilling liquids on himself and being frightened of wild animals. A smile lit up Daisy's face, followed by giggles. She clutched her side with one arm as she laughed.

"Have you seen enough yet?" asked Lara, rubbing her hands together. "It's freezing!"

They returned to the table and finished their meals. Lara passed Tom back his phone with a grateful smile. Daisy led the conversation, asking Logan about his filming days and making jokes with Rufus. Logan was astonished at the transformation whilst remaining oblivious to its cause.

Soon it was time for the museum to close and the group left the restaurant.

Humphrey was waiting for them at the back door, wringing his hands.

Barney growled softly. Lara looked at him in surprise, but before she had the chance to react, Humphrey was waving them inside.

"The last visitor has just left," said Humphrey. "Come on in!"

He led the way into a corridor and through a side door out into the museum. Large old-fashioned double-decker buses lined the outside of the large exhibition room, as well as smaller artefacts.

Barney started sniffing the ground and led Lara in one direction. The others followed.

"Is everything here?" Tom asked Humphrey. "Or is there another storage space?" It was hard to imagine any hiding place being concealed in the big open area of the museum.

"There's various storage areas both in this building and around the country," said Humphrey. His mobile phone started bleeping in his pocket and he took a moment to look at it. "I'll be back in a jiff!"

He scurried back through the side door.

"Vroom vroom!" yelled Rufus, who had climbed into the driver's seat of one of the big red old-fashioned buses. Daisy stood next to him and honked the horn.

Logan stepped inside the bus. "Rufus, don't get us kicked out before we've had a chance to look round."

Tom, Lara and Barney joined the others on-board.

"Do you think there could be a clue hidden on these buses?" asked Rufus, before noticing the worried looks on Lara and Tom's faces. "What's up?"

"Barney was growling…" said Lara. "Something seems off."

Tom's eyes were fixed on the door, which had a glass panel in the top half.

"Quick," he hissed, turning to the others. "Hide!"

Coming through the door were Humphrey and a group of ten men and women, including Frances and Sebastian Battenbridge.

Chapter 16
Hide

The Battenbridge siblings and their employees circled the museum.

"Where are they, Humphrey?" asked Frances in a deep voice that made the hairs on Rufus' arms stand straight. She strutted around the museum floor in a bright red trouser suit and high heels.

"Erm, erm, they were, er, right here," bumbled Humphrey.

"There's only about ten of them," whispered Rufus to Logan. "Can't you beat them up?"

Logan raised his head above the passenger window for a split second and crouched back down. "Negative."

"But you've been going to the gym," protested Rufus, poking one of Logan's muscular arms.

"Doesn't make me James Bond!"

"So disappointing," said Daisy as she shook her head.

"Never mind that… they're blocking the door," said Lara, holding onto Barney's collar.

"They're in here!" yelled one of the men, peering into the bus windows.

Lara let go of Barney and he flew towards the open door, launching himself at two men. They fell backwards onto the floor as Barney leapt back into the bus to defend his friends, barking wildly.

"Why did you let that brute in here?" screamed Frances.

"It was, er, it was the only way they'd come in," stuttered Humphrey as he backed away from the bus.

Barney fended off three more of the Battenbridges' crew, knocking them down like dominoes.

"Enough of this," said Sebastian, his eyes as cold as steel. "Humphrey, fetch my gun from the office."

"B-b-but you can't shoot a dog!"

"Fetch it now before I get it myself and turn it on you."

Humphrey gasped and then hurried off.

Lara turned to the others, her eyes wild with panic. Tom was tinkering under the steering wheel. He cut a cable and pulled some of the plastic away, exposing bare wires.

"Just one more…" he said to himself as he worked on the other end of the cable. "That's it!"

Tom joined the ends of the wires together and the old bus engine crackled into life, sending a pile of smoke from the ancient exhaust directly into Frances Battenbridge's face.

Frances flapped her arms. "Pah! Pah! Sebastian!"

Logan hopped into the driver's seat and steered the bus around the museum floor in a circle. Lara pulled the passenger door shut and locked it from the inside.

"We can't keep going in a circle," said Daisy, looking through the back window of the bus, "they'll catch up with us!"

"Where am I supposed to go?" Logan shrieked, gritting his teeth.

"Why are you steering around them?" yelled Rufus. "Run them over!"

Logan drove straight towards Frances and three of her helpers, who all jumped out of the way and fell to the ground.

Frances staggered to her feet. "Get them *off* my bus!"

A crashing sound caught everyone's attention. Sebastian was running alongside the back of the bus, smashing the windows with a crowbar. Daisy threw herself back towards the front of the bus as glass flew to the ground.

Lara pulled Barney far away from the broken glass. "You need to go faster!"

"Head over there," said Tom, pointing to the back of the museum. Another exhibit was closed off with a criss-crossed metal barrier.

"It's blocked," said Logan.

Rufus grabbed hold of the back of a seat. "Put your foot down!"

Logan slammed his foot down on the accelerator.

"Ahhhhhhhhhhhh!" he hollered, closing his eyes at the last second before the old red bus smashed through the barrier.

"Yesssss!" exclaimed Lara, Daisy and Tom.

Rufus ran to the back of the bus and pointed at Sebastian, who was still chasing after them followed by the others. "In your face!"

"We're not out yet," warned Lara. She moved to the front of the bus and helped guide Logan around the museum's vehicles on display.

"There has to be a way out," said Tom, "all these cars and buses got in."

Lara pointed to a closed garage door. "There it is!"

"One of you is going to have to open it," said Logan, "and fast."

"I'll do it," said Tom, unlocking the passenger door.

Logan screeched the bus to a stop. Tom jumped out and pushed a big red emergency button. The museum door started to slide upwards with a grinding sound and Tom jumped back into the bus, locking the door behind him.

Daisy and Lara looked over their shoulders to see Sebastian pelting towards them. He ran to the passenger door and pulled it, snarling and grunting. He lifted his crowbar but by this time the metal door was almost at the ceiling. Logan accelerated the bus through the space into a side street of Covent Garden.

Shoppers plodded along the road as Logan tooted the bus' horn.

"They're still chasing us," said Lara.

"This must be the slowest getaway vehicle in history," moaned Rufus, staring through his fingers as people casually crossed the street, oblivious to the heavy bus chugging towards them.

"They're catching up with us!" cried Lara, her eyes fixed behind them.

Tom leaned over Logan's arms and pushed down the horn. Rufus wound down the passenger door window and stuck his head out.

"Move it, people!"

The crowds looked up at the noisy bus and nosier young boy and took no notice. Sebastian muscled through the crowds behind them, roughly pushing shoppers out of the way.

"We need to do something…" said Lara, thinking quickly. "Logan, have you got any bank notes?"

Logan rolled his eyes. "Why are you kids always trying to take my money?"

"It's not for us! We need to get these crowds blocking the back of the bus."

"I've only got US dollars left, not British money."

"That'll do."

Logan handed his wallet to Lara. She took a wad of one-dollar bills and returned the wallet to him.

Rufus realised what his cousin was about to do. "Let's throw them from the top," he suggested. "More people will see."

The pair and Daisy climbed up the stairs to the second floor of the double-decker bus. They pushed open two windows at the back.

"Free money!" called Rufus, as they flung the dollar bills into the air.

The notes raining down onto the pavement brought gasps from the pedestrians. Men, women and children reached up to catch the green paper notes, while others searched the floor on their hands and knees. The path at the front of the bus started to clear as people ran to see what was going on at the back of the bus.

Sebastian was stuck behind a group of people scanning the floor.

"Get out of my way," he ordered, kicking someone's back.

A man stood up – at over six foot seven, he towered over Sebastian. "Oi, you kicked my back," he said, grinding his right knuckles into his left palm. "I'll teach you some manners, you oily cretin!" Two of Sebastian's gang members pulled their boss away back down the street as the man glared after them.

"We're in the clear," said Lara with a smile as they came back downstairs. "Now we just need to get away from here."

Logan turned through more side streets. "Where are we going? Back to Swindlebrook?"

"We can't turn up home in this!" exclaimed Lara. "It's probably not even taxed and insured."

"It has a full tank of fuel though..." said Tom. "Which is weird, right?"

Lara thought for a moment. "Yeah... those buses probably don't have to be moved very often around the museum floor."

"Hang on..." said Rufus. "When we nearly ran over Frances, she said 'get them off my bus'... maybe they use this to get the treasure away?"

"It'd be so *reckless* though," considered Lara. "Hiding the treasure on a big red bus stored in a public museum?"

"Maybe they just use it at night," said Rufus. "With Humphrey working there, he probably lets them slip it in and out."

Logan stopped for a moment at traffic lights and Tom stepped off the bus. He snapped a photo of the front before jumping back inside.

Daisy watched him in confusion. "What are you doing?"

"Checking the registration number..." Tom replied, tapping into his phone. "This bus is taxed and has a MOT test certificate. There's no reason for that, unless it's in use..."

Lara snapped her fingers. "And owned by the Battenbridges!"

Chapter 17
All Aboard

"So not only have we stolen their papers... we've also stolen their bus," said Rufus, pumping his fist into the air.

"What?" spluttered Logan, who had been busy focusing on the road. "We've stolen their bus? What if they report us to the police? There's CCTV everywhere in London!"

"They can't report us," said Lara. "They've been hiding their bus in a museum so they can put stolen goods inside it from the closed tunnels at Charing Cross. There's no way they want to draw police attention to that."

"Right... right..." said Logan. "But what are we gonna do with this bus?"

"Search it," said Rufus.

Rufus, Daisy and Lara checked each part of the bus, with Barney sniffing around the seats, eager to help.

Tom carefully picked up as many fragments of glass from the floor as he could, placing them in a carrier bag.

Rufus checked under the last seat. "There's nothing," he complained.

"It's not surprising really is it?" said Lara. "They've been running this operation for a long time… they're not going to leave clues on a bus that members of the public get into every day."

Rufus suddenly dashed towards Logan. "We haven't checked the driver's side!" He reached over Logan's body to open the glovebox compartment.

"Gaaah!" Logan shifted to see around Rufus' sandy head of hair. "Will you get your head out of the windscreen!" Tom and Daisy winced.

"Someone's left a phone," yelled Rufus, flapping it in front of Logan's face.

"That's mine!" Logan snatched the phone, which had a picture of Dee on the front screen.

Rufus returned to one of the seats and sat down with a flop, staring at the floor.

"What's that behind your seat?" Tom asked Logan, pointing to what looked like a small cabinet.

"I'll have to get off my seat to open it," said Logan. Rufus jumped up and Logan put out an arm to stop him. "Wait till we get to those lights."

Logan pulled the bus up to the red traffic lights and hopped out of his seat. He pulled a lever to move it forward and opened the compartment behind it.

Tom tried to see past Logan. "Anything in there?"

"Not really," Logan replied, whilst rooting around. "No papers... no phones... just an empty chocolate bar wrapper and a satnav..."

"Give it to me," said Lara, holding out her palm. "Not the chocolate bar wrapper! The GPS."

She took the navigation system and turned it on. There was one bar of battery life left. She clicked *destination*s then *recently found.*

"There's a postcode in here..."

Rufus jumped up and down. "Let's follow it!"

"Does it have a date when it was used?" asked Tom.

Lara pressed the screen several times. "I'm just looking... there is a date. December eighteenth; it was used last night!"

"They must have taken the treasure last night after it was stolen," said Rufus.

Lara handed the GPS device to Tom, who fixed it onto the windscreen for Logan.

"Have you still got the paper we found yesterday?" Lara asked her cousin. "The one with 'CXS' and 'CWR'?"

Rufus searched his pockets and handed a crumpled piece of paper to Lara.

"I get it now…" said Lara, tracing a circle with her fingers.

"Yeah, Churchill's War Rooms and Charing Cross Station," said Rufus. "We already worked out that bit…"

"I meant the bit at the top that says 'The Ring'… I'd assumed it meant a ring of people, you know, like a gang. But it doesn't… it's a ring of locations they use to take the stolen goods to and hide them."

"Cool," said Daisy, rubbing her palms together. "I can't wait to tell my sister about this! She thought she was all that 'cos she's gone skiing with her mate Lola, wait till she hears I'm catching criminals with you guys!" She took her phone out of her pocket and started tapping furiously.

"Noooo!" yelled Rufus and Lara together.

"What?"

"You can't text your sister," said Lara.

"Why not?"

"Because she's got an even bigger mouth than you," said Rufus, as Daisy's mouth opened wide. "No offence."

Lara moved Daisy's hand away from the screen. "Your sister would call your mum, who would call my mum, who would put a stop to this whole thing."

"Yeah, we don't want any responsible adults getting involved," said Rufus.

"Jeepers, guys!" called out Logan from the driver's seat. "You're so insensitive! I am still here, you know."

"Okay, okay," said Daisy, putting her phone away. "But once this is over, I'm telling everyone. Like seriously... I'm going to start my own blog." She smiled and raised her nose in her air.

Rufus folded his arms. "Great, something for us all to look forward to."

"How many numbers on the sheet again?" Tom asked Lara.

"Five. We've found three already... maybe number four's the postcode in the GPS."

The bus chugged along the bustling streets of London, underneath the white Christmas lights that twinkled overhead.

"Number four out of five," said Rufus. "We're getting close!"

Lara thought of how Frances and Sebastian Battenbridge had tried to trap them inside the London Transport Museum to stop them in their search. She shivered as she recalled how Sebastian had threatened Barney.

"Hopefully not too close."

Chapter 18
The Subway

"The battery's dying," warned Logan, as the GPS flashed a red light and emitted a series of bleeps.

"Nooo!" squealed Daisy, looking up from her phone. "We need the next location for my blog!"

Tom jumped up from his seat and copied the postcode from the device into his phone. "It's okay, I've got it on my maps," he said. "I'll give you directions."

"Does it say where we're going?" said Lara.

"Yeah… Crystal Palace Subway."

"The sandwich place?" asked Logan.

"Of course not," said Lara, before blushing pink and looking at Tom. "It's not… is it?"

Tom smiled. "No, the other type of subway." He noticed Logan's expression looked blank. "That goes under roads."

"Shame," said Rufus, rubbing his stomach. "I could use a snack."

Forty-five minutes later, Tom's phone app announced their arrival at Crystal Palace Subway.

"I can't see anything," said Logan, peering to the right.

"Let's park somewhere and go out and have a look," said Lara.

Logan continued driving around Crystal Palace Park until they came to a car park.

"How do I switch the engine off with no key?" he asked. But before Tom could look, Logan had shifted gears and stalled the engine with a clunk.

"That'll do it," said Tom. The six got out.

Logan fiddled with the door as Lara put on Barney's lead. "I guess we can't lock it from the outside."

"At least it's off the main road," said Rufus. "I feel like the Battenbridges might come out here looking for us."

Lara rubbed Barney's back protectively. "I've been thinking about that too. We can't get trapped somewhere with them again, they'll have a gun this time."

"We need a plan," said Rufus. "If we all go down into the subway, we could all get caught. We've got to split up."

"Won't the subway be crowded with people? And there'll be another way out?" asked Daisy.

Tom looked down at his phone. "It says it's closed, permanently. I'm not sure we can even get in."

They walked through a pathway back towards the main road, where they spotted a small padlocked metal gate. Rufus vaulted over it and ran down some steps.

"It's locked," he called back to the others. "Must be the subway."

"Rufus is right," said Tom. "We need a plan. The Battenbridge gang will be on their way soon."

Everyone turned to Rufus, who had hopped back over the gate.

"What?" he said, shrugging his shoulders.

"What's the plan?" asked Logan.

"Why do I have to come up with the plan?"

"You're always coming up with schemes," said Daisy.

"Yeah, school pranks!"

Lara laughed. "Bit too much for you, is it?"

"No, I just need some space."

Rufus crossed the road away from the others and strode up and down the pavement with his hand on his chin, staring intently at the floor.

"Does he always have to come up with stuff on his own?" asked Logan.

"Recently, yeah," said Lara. "He's been known to go to the bathroom for twenty minutes before his pranks at school."

"We might not have twenty minutes," said Logan, his eyes scanning every car that came past in case it contained a member of the Battenbridge gang.

"Rufus!" yelled Daisy. "Think quicker!"

Rufus sighed heavily and stomped back across the road.

"Creativity needs space," he declared, lifting his hands towards the sky.

"What have you come up with?" asked Tom.

"Well not loads in the fifteen seconds I've had to think," said Rufus. "We need to get them to open the subway. Then we need to get them to leave the subway open so we can sneak in there and find a clue to the last location. So, we need a distraction. We'll write a note and slide it under the door down there, so they only see it when they've unlocked the door. The note will say we'll hand over their secret papers if they find us in the park. Then some of us will be hiding in the park ready to distract them while one or two people hide here and sneak in the subway when they're gone."

There were a few moments of silence.

"That's a decent plan to come up with in fifteen seconds," said Logan appreciatively.

"Yeah, not bad," said Lara. "But what if they leave one or two people behind in the subway?"

Rufus shrugged. "We'll just have to chance it."

"I think you should stay with the bus, Logan," said Tom. "We might need to make a quick exit if they're coming after us."

"Great," said Rufus, folding his arms. "Another quick exit in the world's slowest bus."

"How do I get it started again though?" asked Logan.

"You just hotwire it, take the two exposed wires and…" started Tom, before seeing Logan's face drop. "Er, don't worry. I'll hide somewhere near the bus so I can do it. Let's go now."

Tom and Logan walked back towards the bus.

"I'll go over that way," said Daisy, running away from the direction of the car park, leaving Lara, Rufus and Barney.

Rufus patted his pockets. "We need something to write a note on."

Lara opened her backpack and pulled out a small notepad and pen. Leaning on Rufus' back, she scribbled a quick note.

111

Want your secret papers back? Meet us in the park.

She handed Barney's lead to Rufus and darted down the steps. As she pushed the note under the door, she heard Rufus whisper down to her.

"Hurry up, Lara! They're coming!"

Chapter 19
Crystal Palace Park

With her heart pounding in her chest, Lara tiptoed back up the steps and crouched by Rufus and Barney. The sound of footsteps became louder.

"I can't *believe* you left the GPS in the bus," came the voice of Frances Battenbridge, along with the swooshing sound of her handbag hitting Humphrey.

"W-w-well how was I-ow! How was I-oof! How was I supposed to know they'd drive off in it?" Humphrey whined.

"You'd better hope they don't get here before we've gone."

Good, thought Lara. *They've parked somewhere else and haven't seen Logan and the bus yet.*

The winter sun had almost set out of view and Frances, Sebastian and four other members of their gang did not notice the three shadows hopping from the roadside over the brick barrier into the park.

Rufus pointed behind him, indicating to his cousin that he would go and hide. Lara nodded and knelt down close to the top of the subway as the gang descended the steps.

"Make yourself useful and shine a torch on the lock," said Sebastian.

With a loud creak the door swung open.

"What's this?" asked Sebastian.

A few seconds passed.

"Those kids!" Sebastian seethed. "They've been here, and they've got my papers!"

Loud stomping footsteps pounded a couple of steps as Lara froze to the spot, her breath misting in the cold air.

"Where are you going?" asked Frances.

"They're somewhere in this park," yelled Sebastian. "Wait till I find them, I'll pulverise the—"

"Why are we rushing to find them if that's what they want?" said a voice that Lara did not recognise. "Leave them, Sebastian; we need to move the cargo to number five. Pronto."

"I'm not leaving here until I've got those papers back!"

"What did they take anyway?" persisted the unknown voice. "If they had anything that traced back to us, they'd have taken it to the police already."

Lara could not help feeling that whoever was challenging Sebastian was remarkably logical. Fortunately, Sebastian was too pig-headed to listen.

"They're not getting away with it," he said. Footsteps pounded the last few steps and Lara rushed with Barney behind a tree. She peered around to see Sebastian, Frances and their gang moving off in different directions. As she turned her gaze, she saw two figures that remained by the steps to the subway.

Blast, she thought. *I can't get down there while they're there.*

One of the men was talking into his phone. Ten minutes passed, but it felt like an eternity.

I have to find out where they're going, Lara thought. Barney looked at his friend, unsure why she did not just let him off the lead to have some fun chasing the pair.

One of the men waved his arms towards the road and a delivery truck pulled up alongside him. Both men opened the back of the truck, then went down the steps. They climbed the stairs again carefully, this time transporting objects covered in black cloths.

They're taking the treasure! Lara's breath quickened and her heart raced. Unless she could find out where the men were going, they had no more clues to follow and no more GPS postcodes. It was all down to her and Barney. Act now, or the treasure was gone.

Swallowing hard, Lara strode out from behind the tree towards the van. It was now pitch black, but she still felt exposed and vulnerable walking in the open with Barney by her side. As she reached the railings next to the subway she looked down. The driver of the van and the other two men had gone inside to retrieve the next stolen objects. From the light of their torches, Lara could see several pillars decorated with orange and white diamond patterns. The glint of Egyptian gold caught her attention before one of the men draped it in a sheet.

Feeling helpless, Lara watched as the trio made several more trips from the hidden subway to the van. Her hands felt clammy under her gloves despite the cold night breeze as she dreaded the men getting away or worse still, spotting her spying on them with Barney.

"Right," said the driver, after they had placed a particularly large item in the back. "You two can manage that last one."

He climbed up into the driver's seat and started the engine. The remaining two men went down the steps for the last time.

Lara stood up and crept to the back of the van.

Think, think... think of something, she thought desperately. But all she could think of was the men getting away. Seconds passed and the pressure mounted to a peak.

The subway door was slammed shut with a bang that sent Lara's nerves into overdrive.

Barney, what are we going to do? Lara looked at her dog, fearing that she no longer had time to escape back through the park without being seen.

Taking a deep breath, she jumped into the back of the delivery truck.

Chapter 20
The Maze

Meanwhile, Tom was facing some difficult decisions of his own. He needed to distract the gang for as long as possible, to give Lara enough time to explore the subway and find the last clue.

A sign caught his attention – *Crystal Palace Park Maze*. He followed it to find tall hedges opening into a path.

Maybe I could lose them in here, Tom thought to himself. It was risky though; mazes had one way in and out, so if the gang found the right path, they could trap him. He pulled out his phone and searched for an image of the maze. Tracing the picture on his phone with his index finger, he memorised the correct route. Tom was used to map reading for his dad when they had to make their way to agricultural fairs in Cornwall, and he had a strong sense of direction.

He walked back to the sign and saw Sebastian and three others running through the park.

"Over here," Tom yelled, waving his arms. Sebastian turned and pointed at the thirteen-year-old.

"Give me back my papers *now*," he hollered.

Tom sprinted through the maze, navigating the twists and turns under the moonlit sky. He quickly reached the middle which opened up into a large circle.

Keeping perfectly still, Tom waited. He did not want to move too much in case he trod on a branch. For a few minutes, the only sounds were rushing footsteps shuffling, stopping and starting up again as the gang tried one path, came to a dead end and turned around.

"Bill, can't you climb to the top of these hedges?" Tom heard Sebastian mutter in exasperation. "We haven't got all day!"

Tom quietly took a step backwards to stand against the hedge. He hoped that if one of the gang members looked from above, they would not see him. He heard rustling sounds as Bill tried to scale the hedge.

"Oof!" he said after a thud. "Seb mate, this ain't 'alf 'ard!"

"Don't call me Seb… and pronounce the letter 'h'!"

"I can't blinkin' do it! This 'edge is all slippery!"

"Just get on with it."

"You try it!"

"I most certainly will not! You are hired to do a job, now *do it*."

"Weren't 'ired to go climbing up blinkin' 'edges," complained Bill. "Ought to get a raise for this malarkey."

"You ought to get a kick up your backside," said Sebastian, kicking the dirt instead. "Hurry up!"

A series of grunts and grumbling accompanied three more falls to the ground. Finally, Bill reached the top and dangled his torch.

"Well?" asked Sebastian, tapping his feet with his arms folded. "What can you see?"

"What am I looking for? The middle of the maze or the boy?"

"The boy, you fool! I don't care about a stupid maze!"

"Can't see 'im."

"Get down here… I'll look myself."

Tom pressed himself further against the hedge, fearing that Sebastian and Bill were right on the other side of him. Sebastian scrambled up the hedge much quicker than his employee.

Tom held his breath as a light shined into the middle of the maze. It travelled around for a few moments.

"Seb!" whispered Bill as he tugged on Sebastian's trouser leg. "Seb! *Seb*! Can you see the boy?"

Sebastian tried to kick Bill's hand away. "Shut... up!"

Tom's shoulders felt tense as he waited. The torchlight edged closer and closer to his feet.

"There he is!" Sebastian shouted. "Get him!" He lost his grip of the hedge and fell straight on top of Bill.

"Ow! Seb!"

"Come on!" The pair got up and ran to find the entrance to the middle of the maze.

Meanwhile, Tom had darted out of the centre, frantically trying to recall the image of the map in his mind. Footsteps from Sebastian, Bill and two more of the gang sounded alarmingly close.

Right, right, left, Tom thought to himself as he pelted through the maze. *Three more turns... two more turns...*

Tom stopped in shock as he turned and came face to face with Sebastian, who lunged forward to grab the boy's shoulder and missed as Tom jumped back.

"We've got you now," said Sebastian, as two more men approached from the other direction, blocking Tom's escape route. "Hand over the papers!"

"Okay, okay," said Tom, holding his hands up. "Let me get them out of my backpack."

Tom opened his backpack. As he glanced down at the bag in front of him, he noticed a tiny gap at the bottom of the hedge by his right foot. He yanked out some papers he had printed from the internet on 'Festive Things to Do in London' and threw them in the air.

"Hey!" cried Sebastian as Tom dived under the gap in the hedge.

Tom was almost through when he felt a firm hand grasping his ankle. He wriggled and struggled as he was pulled backwards.

"I've got you!" said Sebastian.

Taking a deep breath, Tom kicked as fast as he could. Sebastian's grip loosened for a split second and Tom was free. He raced back to the car park, with one shoe on and one left in Sebastian's hand.

Chapter 21
The Dinosaurs

When he left Lara and Barney, Rufus ran past the car park to an area with a lake. He shone his torch and saw a surprising sight in front of him – a series of large model dinosaurs lined the park and the water's edge.

"So cool!" Rufus marvelled as he approached one of the figures. Studying dinosaurs and fossils at school had been one of the few lessons he had enjoyed.

Rufus explored the area and the gigantic prehistoric replicas, until he had almost forgotten that the Battenbridge gang would soon be looking for him. He was reminded when he heard the sound of bickering coming from a man and a woman approaching the lake.

"This is all your fault for letting them get away in the first place," said a voice that unmistakably belonged to Frances Battenbridge.

"That's not fair," moaned Humphrey. "How was I to know they'd hotwire a bus and escape out the museum?"

"With our satnav." Frances shook her head. "You really are a nincompoop, Humphrey, on multiple levels."

Humphrey muttered and grumbled as they looked around the park.

"They're not here," said Frances as they turned to go.

"Over here," yelled Rufus, waving his hands and shining a torch from the other side of the water. He had to distract them for a while, so they did not find Lara and Barney by the subway entrance.

"Get him!" shrieked Frances. The pair hurried around the water's edge as Rufus disappeared through the trees and moved the other way around the lake. He crouched behind one of the dinosaurs.

Humphrey swung around, looking in every direction. "Where did he go?"

"Why are you asking me? Look for him!"

"Ahoy!" shouted Rufus as he popped his head up from behind the dinosaur statue and ducked back down.

"For pity's sake, Humphrey, hurry up before he moves!"

Humphrey shuffled around to the other side of the lake followed by Frances, who was making slower progress in her high-heeled stiletto boots.

"Humphrey, if you go any slower, you'll stop," said Frances, as she stopped to un-wedge her heel from the mud.

"Well you're not helping—" Humphrey stopped talking when he saw Frances looking as if she were going to fling her boot at him.

"Raaaarrrrr!" screeched a voice from the entrance to the dinosaur park that took Frances, Humphrey and even Rufus by surprise.

"Did you hear that?" said Humphrey, clutching Frances' arm.

"Of course I did, worthless! Get over there! It must be another of those awful children."

Daisy was bent double with laughter, her sides shaking. When she had recovered, she put her hands to her mouth and released another dinosaur screech.

Humphrey stopped dead in his tracks as Frances ploughed into him.

"Keep going, Humphrey!"

"Hurry up, I'm getting bored," called Rufus from the opposite direction, where he had climbed up into a tree.

"Go, go!" Frances gave Humphrey a shove.

Rufus disappeared at once.

"This is no good, Frances. He's too ruddy quick! We'll have to split up – you go one way after one kid and I'll go the other, then we'll corner them."

"Fine."

The pair moved off in separate directions and began searching around the lake, looking around the dinosaur objects. As Humphrey edged closer to Rufus' hiding spot behind a rock, Rufus watched his position, waiting for the opportune moment.

"Raaaaaaar!" Roaring like a delinquent dinosaur, Rufus flung himself towards Humphrey and pushed him straight into the lake. Humphrey's belly flop caused a big splash.

"Help, help!" he cried, thrashing his arms about. Rufus disappeared back into the darkness. "Frances! Frances! I can't swim! Help me, Frances!"

"No." Frances inspected her fake fingernails to check that her nail polish was still in place.

"But… Frances!" spluttered Humphrey as he spat out water. "I need help!"

"Pull yourself together, you hog." Frances continued looking around the lake.

"Y-y-you can't leave me h-h-here! I'll drown!"

"You'll have to get yourself out. These boots are *designer*."

"I-I-I don't know how long I can hold myself above water!"

Frances sighed loudly and moved slowly to where Humphrey was half-drowning.

"You really are about as useful as a chocolate teapot." Frances picked up a log and threw it in the water.

"W-w-what am I supposed to— blah!" Water was entering Humphrey's mouth at an alarming rate. "What am I supposed to do with that?"

"Float on it, you imbecile!"

"It's alre— blah! It's already sunk!"

Daisy found Rufus and crouched next to him. The pair stifled their giggles behind a dinosaur statue.

Frances found a longer branch and held one end of it towards Humphrey.

"Grab it, buffoon!"

Humphrey swung his arms wildly, trying and failing to grab the stick. Frances leaned forward to get more reach. As she did so, Rufus and Daisy spotted another opportune moment. They gave each other a quick nod.

"Raaaaarrrr!" came a dual cry. Frances turned and screamed, but it was too late. In half a second she had splashed into the water next to Humphrey.

Rufus and Daisy high-fived each other with huge grins. Humphrey gratefully grabbed hold of his boss for support, unwittingly pushing her head underwater with his weight.

Frances struggled for a few seconds before bursting above water and gasping for breath.

"How *dare* you," she screamed, black mascara and purple eyeshadow smeared over her soaking face.

"We gotta get out of here," said Rufus, between giggles. The pair ran out of the dinosaur exhibit. "Thanks, guys," Rufus said, nodding at a large toothy dinosaur on their way out.

Chapter 22
Back on the Bus

Rufus and Daisy sped back to the car park where Logan was waiting with the bus. They hopped on-board.

"Where are the others?" asked Logan.

Rufus bent over, trying to catch his breath. "Lara... and Barney... are at the subway entrance. I didn't see where Tom went."

They waited, Logan becoming increasingly fidgety as the minutes passed.

A figure came running towards them.

"Who is it?" asked Logan, squinting. "Friend or foe?"

Daisy squinted. "It's Tom!"

"Phew," sighed Logan in relief.

Tom jumped onto the bus and started the engine for Logan.

"We've got to go and get Lara and Barney," he said. "The gang are coming after us, now!" Logan reversed the bus and turned out of the car park.

"Did you see Frances and Humphrey?" Tom asked Rufus.

"Yeah we did," sniggered Daisy.

"They made a *splash* alright!" said Rufus, nudging Daisy with his elbow, before looking down at Tom's foot. "Hey, where's your shoe?"

"In Sebastian's hand."

Logan drove round to the subway entrance.

"Where are they?" he asked, peering through the window.

"She should hear us," said Tom as the bus engine chugged noisily.

A few moments passed and Tom began to drum his hands on the dashboard as his eyes darted across the park. He got out of the passenger door and went over to the steps leading to the subway.

"Lara," he whispered. "Lara, you there?" He tried again, raising his voice. "Lara! Lara!"

Rufus and Daisy joined Tom and whistled loudly for Barney. There was no response, and the only sounds were the traffic on the streets and an owl hooting in the distance.

Tom jumped back into the park and shone his torch.

"Tom! I can hear Sebastian!" whispered Rufus. A second later Sebastian and Bill came into view, running towards them at speed.

"Lara!" called Tom urgently.

"She's not here," said Rufus, pulling Tom by the arm back towards the bus. "We've got to go!"

Tom resisted, desperate to find his missing friends.

"Come *on*," urged Daisy, taking Tom's other arm. "We can't find them if we get caught." They pulled Tom back on-board.

Rufus slammed the door shut. "Drive, Logan!"

"Where's Lara and Barney?"

"They're not here but the gang are coming, *go!*"

Logan put his foot down and the bus chugged away from Crystal Palace Park. Tom sat on the floor by the door, his head in his hands.

Chapter 23
Where are Lara and Barney?

"She'll kill me," said Logan in a trembling voice. "Sarah Jacobs is going to kill me. That's if Dee doesn't do it first! How did we lose them?"

"Wait..." said Rufus. "Two people followed me into the dinosaur park – Frances and Humphrey. How many people followed you, Tom?"

"Two," answered Tom in a quiet voice, his hands still covering his face.

"There were six people that came to the subway. So, unless two people were looking somewhere else... they might have stayed back at the subway entrance."

"Kidnapped!" yelped Logan. "What are we gonna do? We need to call the police!"

Rufus tapped Logan's arm. "Calm down! Barney wouldn't let Lara get kidnapped."

Tom raised his head.

"Think about it... he'd never let them take Lara," Rufus continued.

"But what if they hurt Barney?" Daisy asked, swallowing hard.

"Then he'd still be in the park."

Tom considered this for a moment.

"So, if they're somewhere together..." he said, looking up. "Where did they go?"

"I don't know..."

"We *need* to go to the police," insisted Logan.

"And tell them what?" said Rufus. "We stole some papers and a bus, and now we can't find Lara?"

"But we lost her!"

"Well..." said Rufus, breaking a few awkward moments of silence. "Tom lost his shoe."

"I lost my *niece*!" exclaimed Logan, waving one hand wildly. "That is not the same as losing a shoe!"

"Calm down, it was a *joke*," said Rufus.

"Not a very funny one," said Tom quietly.

Daisy wrung her hands as she took a seat. "I wish she had a phone."

Logan's phone began vibrating in his pocket. With a fumbling hand he fished it out and glanced at the screen.

"Gaaaah!" he squealed, dropping his phone on the floor. "It's Sarah! Rufus, you speak to her."

Rufus stared at him, wide-eyed. "What? No! You do it!"

"I'm driving!"

Rufus sighed and picked up the phone from the floor.

"Hi Auntie Sarah," he said, in a cheery voice.

"Rufus, where's Logan?"

"We're on a bus," Rufus replied, feeling grateful that his aunt did not ask to speak to Lara.

"Oh. I wondered what time you're all coming home?"

"Soon... ish," said Rufus. "We're stuck in traffic though, then we need to get the train, so it could be a... while?"

"Well, call me when you're on the train. We've got visitors coming later and I want you all to be here. Have you had dinner?"

"Not yet... but I think we'll get something here before we get the train."

"Well don't leave it too long. Have you all had a nice day?"

"Smashing, brilliant," said Rufus, a little too quickly. "Best be off then, see you later, Auntie Sarah!"

"But wa—"

"Bye!"

Rufus ended the call and sighed.

"Did she guess?" asked Logan, biting the fingernails on his right hand as he held the steering wheel with his left.

"Of course not!" said Rufus, rolling his eyes. "How would she guess that we've been on the trail of treasure thieves for two days and that Lara and Barney have gone missing?"

"I don't know… and I don't know where I'm going. We need to go to a police station now. I'm not having my niece in danger; this has gone far enough."

"Okay," said Tom, tapping into his phone. "Let's go to Charing Cross Police Station. Lara has our phone numbers, if we don't hear from her by then we'll go in and report everything."

"Just breathe," said Daisy, standing next to Logan demonstrating. "Expand your chest."

"Okay," said Logan, taking big gulps of air. "And… calm…"

The rest of the bus journey was not very calm for Logan, Daisy, Rufus and Tom. They hit a traffic jam on the road back into central London that brought the bus to a standstill.

"I can't handle this," said Logan, who looked as if he had aged a few years during the bus ride. "Shall we just call the police instead?"

"No!" said Rufus. "Stick to the plan!"

Logan wound the windows down and flapped his shirt.

After an hour and a half of crawling through traffic, Logan found a place to park and the trio walked up the steps of Charing Cross Police Station.

"I still think we should give it more time," said Rufus. "I really think they're alright."

"No," said Logan. "We need to do the right thing. I've stuffed it up enough already with you kids."

Logan placed his hand on the door handle and walked into the police station.

Chapter 24
Lara and Barney's Journey

While Tom had been running through the Crystal Palace Park maze and Rufus was hiding in various spots around the dinosaur exhibition, Lara and Barney were travelling in the back of a van, concealed under one of the blankets the men had used to hide the treasure.

"If Mum let me have a phone, I could call someone right now," Lara whispered to Barney as she stroked his fur. "And I could track where we're going! This is *so* annoying."

The van felt like it was travelling fast. Lara lifted off the blanket and reached into her backpack.

"At least you can have your dinner," she said, pulling an enormous dog chew out of her bag for Barney. He took it from her hand gratefully. Lara grabbed a small metal dish and a bottle of water from her belongings. She took a couple of swigs of water before pouring the rest into the dish for Barney. He licked her hands before diving into the bowl.

"What am I going to do?" Lara asked Barney, after he had wolfed down his dog chew and lapped up all the water. He looked up at her with adoring eyes.

"It was stupid of us to get in here, Barney! We still don't know where they're taking the treasure."

Lara pressed her ear against the metal that separated them from the two gang members in the front. She strained hard, but all she could hear was a power ballad from the eighties blaring out from the van's radio. Every now and then, one of the gang members would sing along, badly and out of tune.

"Urgh," said Lara with a shudder, moving away from the divider.

She hunted around the van looking for clues, with Barney sniffing the different objects. There was only the stolen Egyptian treasure covered in the sheets. Lara turned her attention to the back of the van.

I can unlock this from the inside, she thought, as she ran her hand along the lock mechanism. She pulled the handle and opened the door slightly. They were on the motorway with other cars speeding by. She quickly slammed the door shut and held her breath to see if the two men in the front had noticed. Luckily, they were too absorbed in warbling power ballads to notice.

"When the van stops, we need to run," Lara told Barney as she sat back down next to him. "We have to get out of here as soon as possible and call Tom or Logan."

Barney nuzzled his head into Lara's arm.

Lara waited on tenterhooks for an opportunity to escape the van. Every time the vehicle slowed, she was ready to pounce on the lock, but several times it sped up again. She had no idea how long they had been waiting inside or what time it was.

Feeling exhausted, she started to doze off, her head resting against Barney's fur.

Stay awake, she thought to herself, as she jolted awake for the fifth time.

After what felt like a decade, the van began to slow again. She waited, expecting it to speed up again, but this time the engine was switched off. Her heart beating wildly, she slung her backpack over her shoulder and fumbled with the lock. It swung open onto the two startled men. Lara jumped through the middle of them followed by Barney and pelted down the hill.

"Hey!" yelled one of the men, as they both started to give chase.

Lara had never run so fast in her life, her feet pounded the pavement and she did not dare to look behind her. She heard the two men's footsteps getting closer and gritted her teeth as she charged forward with Barney.

They continued down a hillside. Lara had no idea where they were running in the dark, lamp-lit streets, but smelt sea air. They passed a stone building on the right-hand side with windows lit, but the men were too close for her to risk approaching the building's occupants for help.

As they got to the bottom of the hill, Lara started to feel the sharp pang of stitch in her stomach. She gasped for air and persevered through the agony that was increasing with every step.

They entered a town, with white buildings on either side. Desperate to lose the two men without trapping themselves in a dead end, Lara turned into a side street. She took a sharp left into another street then another. For the first time the men were out of view and she dived into the first open shop she could see, ducking down with Barney behind the window.

The two men ran past and began to slow down as they looked around them.

"Hey! Get that dog out of here!"

Lara turned to see a woman in her early twenties standing in a pizza takeaway shop behind a counter.

"Please, I need help…" Lara gasped, exhausted from her escape. "Two men are chasing me!"

The woman's scowl softened. "Are you alright?"

"Yeah… please may I use your phone?"

The woman pushed a cordless phone across the counter.

Lara pulled her notebook from her bag where she kept the phone numbers of her family and best friends. She dialled Logan's number.

"Hello?" Tom answered in a concerned voice.

"Tom, it's me."

"Lara!" Tom's voice was full of relief. "Where are you? Are you alright?"

Lara paused for a moment. She still had no idea where she was.

"What town is this?" she asked the lady, whose tag on her shirt spelt the name Priya.

"Dover," Priya responded, raising an eyebrow.

"Did you hear that?" Lara continued to Tom. "Where are you guys?"

"At the police station, we haven't gone in to speak to anyone yet. Do you want us to get down there to you? Are you and Barney alright?"

"We're fine," said Lara, not wanting to say too much in front of Priya. "I can get the train back up to Swindlebrook and meet you there… it'll be quicker. But

141

wait—" Lara searched inside her purse as she leant the phone against her ear.

"I don't think I've got enough money on me."

"Wait there… I can book you one online and tell you the ticket code. There's a train to Swindlebrook at seven o'clock… twenty minutes away. Can you make that?"

"How far is the station from here?" Lara asked Priya.

"A couple of miles… Ryan can give you a lift, but I want to talk to an adult on there to make sure everything's alright."

"Tom, put Logan on," said Lara. "He's my uncle," she explained to Priya, handing across the phone.

"Hi… you're her uncle, yeah?… What's going on, why's your niece being chased by two blokes? Okay… okay… right… you're *the* Logan Jacobs? …From *Logan's Jungle Trek*? Seriously? Yeah, yeah, it's no trouble, Ryan can give her a lift… okay, yeah, alright, ta ta then, I'll hand you back to your niece."

Priya handed the phone back to Lara with a huge grin on her face.

"Logan Jacobs," she said to herself as she went out the back to find Ryan.

"Lara, Tom's bought a ticket on his phone, I'll give you the code…"

Lara scribbled the reference in her notepad and hung up the phone.

A couple of minutes later, Lara was in the passenger seat next to Ryan the pizza delivery driver, with Barney on the back seat staring out of the window.

"Are you sure you'll be alright from here?" Ryan asked as they arrived at Dover Priory Station.

"We'll be fine," Lara assured him. "I've got my ticket code. Thank you for your help."

Lara collected her ticket and used the change in her bag to buy a sandwich and another bottle of water. Soon she was on the train with Barney snoozing at her feet, passing fields and villages in the dark December night as the train hurtled towards Swindlebrook.

Chapter 25
Reunions

It was half past eight by the time that everyone trooped up to the front door. Logan had driven the bus from London to meet Lara at Swindlebrook Station. They left it two blocks away from Mrs Jacobs' house to avoid questions on why they had turned up late in a vintage bus with smashed out windows at the back.

Lara's mum opened the door before they could ring the doorbell.

"*Finally*," she said with her arms folded. "We've been waiting ages."

"Who's *we*?" asked Lara.

"I told you all when I phoned five times this evening that we had visitors waiting."

Rufus gave his cousin a nudge.

"Oh yeah," said Lara, blushing as she avoided direct eye contact with her mum. "So you did."

Mrs Jacobs looked at Tom's feet. "Where's your shoe?"

"Err... it got stuck." Tom looked at the floor.

"My mum's spotted me," said Daisy, as a thumping came from the kitchen window across the street. "Text me!" She gave Lara's arm a squeeze and skipped across the street to her house.

Barney rushed inside past Mrs Jacobs and a series of squeals and giggling erupted.

"Maye!" exclaimed Lara, stepping forward. Their Egyptian friend was rolling around the hallway floor with Barney, who was barking in delight. She got up and pulled her friends into a group hug.

"What are you doing here?" asked Rufus.

"Me and my mother and father are staying with Karim on holiday."

"We just arrived in London today," said Karim, joining the others in the hall. "I've been in Cairo for two weeks, so I couldn't make the awards lunch."

They moved towards the living room where the third visitor was seated on the couch.

"Dee!" Logan hugged his girlfriend in the most awkward embrace Lara had ever seen. "But you were in LA?"

Dee's face broke into a huge smile.

"We got the TV deal!"

"You got the deal?" Logan grinned before his face dropped. "But they weren't interested before... they came around after I left?"

"Sounds about right," murmured Lara to Tom.

"Hold up—" interrupted Rufus. Everyone turned to look at him as he sniffed the air like a golden retriever. "Someone's been eating pizza!"

"Calm down, Rufus, there's some in the kitchen but you'll have to heat it up in—"

Before Mrs Jacobs had completed her sentence Rufus was already in the kitchen, followed closely by Barney and Logan.

The group spent an enjoyable evening catching up and reminiscing about their adventure in Egypt a couple of months ago. Mrs Jacobs shuddered at some of the stories of the peril they had got into.

"Thank goodness we're having such a nice peaceful Christmas break," she said.

Her statement was met with silence before Rufus, Lara and Tom hastily nodded their agreement.

A few minutes later, Dee and Logan were alone in the kitchen.

"You've not updated me since you needed the Charing Cross Station film pass – and Sarah doesn't know anything about it," Dee said, her eyebrows raised in accusation. "You're in danger, aren't you? That's why you're not being open with Sarah."

Logan hung his head low as he reached for a Diet Coke out of the fridge.

"I can't talk about it," he said.

"Don't be a pillock! Tell me what's going on."

Logan sighed.

"Dee, this is *big*. This gang's been stealing treasure for decades and hiding it in a ring of different locations around London."

"I *knew* it!" cried a voice behind the pair. Dee and Logan turned to see Maye standing in the doorway, stroking Barney's fur. "I knew you were all up to something! Where are we going to catch the criminals?"

"We are not going anywhere," whispered Logan, closing the door behind Maye and Barney. "This is not your concern."

"I'll just tell Mrs Jacobs then," said Maye, turning towards the living room.

"No!" cried Logan, putting a hand on the door.

Dee stepped between them. "Why not? She has a right to know."

Maye nodded vigorously. "Yeah, I do."

"Not you! Sarah."

"You heard her out there," said Logan with a shrug. "She wants a nice peaceful Christmas holiday; she doesn't want to be dealing with criminals."

Rufus, Lara and Tom joined them in the kitchen.

"She probably doesn't want the kids to be dealing with criminals either," Dee retorted.

"Urgh, a responsible adult!" said Rufus, slapping his hands on his forehead.

"Someone has to be! So, where's the treasure now?"

"Somewhere in Dover," said Lara. "If I looked at a map, I might be able to find the pizza place and work out where the van stopped..."

"Here," said Tom, tapping into his phone app to search for pizza places in Dover. Lara leaned across and moved the screen with her fingers.

"There," she said, pointing. "And we ran from that direction down a hill... Dover Castle. That's where they stopped the van, it's got to be the last location in the ring!"

"Well Dover is the closest they can get to France," said Dee. "Maybe that's the last hiding place before they take the goods out of the country."

The kitchen door opened, and Mrs Jacobs walked in with Karim.

"Dover?" Mrs Jacobs looked at the screen over Lara's shoulder. "Why are you looking there?"

"We're going to Dover Castle tomorrow," said Maye as she hugged her own waist.

"Tomorrow?" Mrs Jacobs knitted her eyebrows. "Karim and I have to be on a conference call tomorrow morning, it's the last one before the Christmas break. I was hoping we could all do something together in the afternoon?"

"We'll need most of the day to have a proper look, Auntie Sarah," said Rufus. "Let's do something together in the evening. And we've still got two days left before Tom goes back to Cornwall."

"Please," begged Maye. "I've never seen a castle before." She looked at Mrs Jacobs with wide eyes.

"Perhaps I can come here early tomorrow with Maye," suggested Karim. "Then she can go to Dover with the others while we take the project call from here."

"Alright, as long as that's okay with you two to go with the kids to Dover?" Mrs Jacobs glanced at Dee and Logan.

"Well…" said Dee, as everyone's faces turned to her. Rufus was standing behind Mrs Jacobs and Karim silently mouthing the word 'please' and placing his hands together. Barney sat in front of Dee and lifted a paw.

"O…kay…" she said slowly, shuffling her feet.

149

"Yes!" cried Lara, Rufus, Tom and Maye.

"Come on now, Maye, we need to get back to London," said Karim, putting a hand around his little sister's shoulder. "Thank you for the pizza, Sarah. Goodnight everyone! See you tomorrow."

Chapter 26
Dover

Karim and Maye arrived early the next morning, shortly followed by Dee who had returned to her house the evening before.

"Another adventure," whispered Maye, giving Tom a friendly punch on his arm. She was bundled in a thick coat, hat, scarf and gloves, with furry boots.

"You look toasty," said Lara.

"It's so cold," Maye replied as she rubbed her gloves together. "I've never been anywhere so cold! It's going to snow!"

"Nah," said Rufus. "It never snows in Britain in December."

Daisy spotted the group from her window and ran out the front door.

"Who's this one?" asked Dee.

"My friend Daisy," said Lara, putting her arm around Daisy's shoulder. "This is our friend Maye from Egypt and this is Dee."

"Hi." Daisy smiled at them both.

"We won't all fit in one car," said Dee after they had said goodbye to Mrs Jacobs and Karim. "Are we going to get the train?"

"To the bus!" yelled Rufus, charging up the road.

"There's a bus going to Dover?" questioned Dee.

Logan rubbed the back of his neck. "Well… we're driving our own bus at the moment."

"A minibus?"

"Err, yeah, no, it's this way."

Logan followed Rufus to the space a few streets along where they had parked the bus.

"Where on earth did you get this?" asked Dee as she inspected the outside of the vehicle.

"It's on loan from the British Transport Museum," said Rufus.

"Who smashed these?" Dee pointed to the back windows.

"One of the people who's been stealing the treasure," replied Logan.

Dee placed her hands on her hips. "Is it safe for us to go after these people?"

"We're just going to have a look around the castle," said Rufus. "It'll be fine. And we've got Barney."

They got on-board and Tom started up the bus for Logan.

"Why are you hot-wiring it?" asked Dee. "I feel like there's stuff you're not telling me!"

"Er, because we don't have the key," said Tom.

"I want to go up the top!" shouted Maye as she ran up the stairs. Tom, Rufus, Daisy, Lara and Barney joined her. Logan set off for Dover with Dee asking him a series of awkward questions.

"I've been looking it up," said Tom, holding his phone. "Dover Castle has miles of underground tunnels; they were used in World War Two."

"The treasure must've been taken there then," said Lara. "The castle wouldn't have enough hiding places since tourists can go in there."

"The tunnels are open to visitors as well, but only a bit of them."

"Do they allow dogs?" Lara asked.

"No…" answered Tom, scrolling his phone. "It says only guide dogs."

"I'll ask Dee, maybe she can get us another filming pass." Lara got up to walk down to the bottom deck.

"The return of *Trainbusters*!" yelled Rufus, pumping his fist in the air.

"I need to know everything," said Maye. "You didn't tell me much last night."

"Same here," added Dee, who had followed Lara back upstairs. "I already asked my colleague to get us a pass, he's emailing a letter through. But tell me everything."

Lara, Tom, Daisy and Rufus told Dee and Maye their story, from the lunch at the Egyptologists' Society, to confronting the Battenbridge siblings at Churchill's War Rooms and stealing their papers, to the underground platforms at Charing Cross Station, escaping from the London Transport Museum in a vintage bus and hiding from their enemies in Crystal Palace Park.

"So these guys know you've been trailing them around London and they know that Lara and Barney got in their van to Dover last night?" said Dee. "We're going to have to be really careful."

About an hour and a half later, the bus arrived in Dover. The sky was almost as white as the chalk cliffs that rose up from the sea.

It was only half past eight as Logan parked the bus in the town centre and they walked up to the castle.

"I'm afraid we're not open for over an hour," said a lady in a thick woollen coat by the entrance. "And we don't allow dogs, unfortunately."

"We've got an appointment," said Dee, taking out her phone and showing the lady an email. "We're planning on filming a documentary here soon and we need to check out the tunnels before we bring the crew down."

"Wait a moment…" said the lady, her eyes brightening as she spotted Logan. "You're not that chap from—"

"*Logan's Jungle Trek*, yep it's him, Logan Jacobs, international adventurer, TV star, blah blah blah," said Rufus.

"Oh *my*." The lady put her hand on her chest.

"I can't believe that used to be me," whispered Daisy to Lara.

"My grandchildren will be delighted to hear about this!"

Logan hung back to talk to the lady while the others moved ahead.

"How many times has that happened?" asked Maye.

"*Too* many," said Lara, looking over her shoulder. Logan was talking animatedly to his new fan whilst running a hand through his brown locks. "Look at him, he lives for this stuff."

They walked from the visitor centre down to two entrances to the underground tunnels. One was sign-posted as a hospital and the other, 'Operation Dynamo'.

"They're open," said Rufus, running down the hill.

"Wait, young man," called out the lady. "We need to get you a tour guide first."

"Oh, no need, Doris," said Logan, putting a hand on the lady's back. "After trekking the Himalayas on *Logan's Jungle Trek*, I can lead everyone around alright."

"Good grief," muttered Dee, shaking her head.

Doris giggled.

"Still… I think I ought to get someone to guide you. Ted should be around here somewhere…"

"But we want to get the *feel* of the place," insisted Logan. "It's so important for my TV shows to be authentic… you know what I mean?"

"Well not really, no…"

"I have to rely just on myself when I'm out in the wild…"

"With local guides, a film crew and multiple food deliveries," Dee added under her breath.

156

"…So, I like to lead myself around a new location. Don't worry, we'll just have a quick scoot around before the public starts coming in and then we'll have a nice cup of tea in the restaurant."

"Alright…" Doris conceded. "You've not got long though so just a quick look and you must keep to the designated visitor paths."

"Thank you." Logan flashed his sparkling white teeth at Doris and joined the others.

"Which one do we try?" asked Tom, staring at the two entrances.

"Maybe they both join up somewhere," said Lara.

Barney turned to look at both entrances then pulled Lara on his lead towards the underground hospital.

"I guess the hospital it is!"

Chapter 27
The Underground Hospital

Barney led the way through the underground hospital. Passing through numerous corridors with metal corrugated walls, they entered wards lined with beds and an operating room kitted out with surgical instruments.

Lara shivered. "It feels eerie."

"Is this still a hospital?" asked Maye.

"No, it's a museum display," said Tom. "We need to find the part of the tunnels that's closed to the public."

They continued down the tunnels.

"This way," said Rufus, opening a door with a no entry sign. Dee, at the back of the group, glanced backwards as she followed.

The corridors continued with more modern storage furniture against the walls. Turning further corners, the tunnel became narrower. They came to another door, again marked no entry. Rufus opened it to reveal an undeveloped part of the tunnels with no metal-ridged shelter walls. The ceiling, floor and walls were carved out from the cliff rocks.

Dee stopped, peering down at pieces of rubble that had fallen on the floor. "Be very careful, everyone."

They moved through the tunnel in single file, following its twists and turns.

"Blocked!" exclaimed Rufus, as they reached a mound of clay-coloured rock.

"I can see a gap!" Before anyone could stop her, Maye dived forward to the top right-hand corner of the blockage into a tiny gap. Barney was behind her in an instant.

"Get out, both of you!" yelled Lara. "It might not be safe!"

Barney leapt back down to the ground and Tom pulled Maye out by her legs.

"Is it a roof fall?" asked Daisy.

Tom put his hand on the clay. "It can't be. This stuff's a completely different colour to the walls and ceiling. Someone blocked it off on purpose."

"It must lead to the hiding place then!" Rufus lifted a foot up to scale the wall.

"Wait!" cried Dee, pulling Rufus back. "Let Logan go first."

"Blimey..." Logan heaved the top half of his body up into the hole. "It's a bit tight," he said, wriggling his bottom.

"Get on with it," called out Dee behind him.

"I'm stuck!"

"Tom, help me push his legs," said Dee. The pair of them took a foot each and shoved.

"Owww! It's not helping! Now I'm even more stuck!"

"Push yourself forward," said Lara.

"Make yourself smaller!" said Maye.

"I can't breathe! Get me out! Get me out!"

Tom and Dee pulled Logan back out of the hole.

"Well that was rubbish," said Rufus, his arms folded.

"I'd like to see you try!"

"Sure." Rufus jumped back into the hole and wriggled along on his tummy, closely followed by Maye, Lara, Barney, Daisy and Tom.

"Wait!" cried Dee. "You can't all go! I can't fit in there either, it's too small!"

"We'll come back later," said Rufus.

"Don't tell me you'll come back later! I've taken responsibility for you kids and you can't just disappear down a hole... Logan, say something!" Dee shoved Logan forward.

"Let us know what's on the other side," he said.

Dee poked him in the chest. "Not helpful!"

Dee's voice became muffled as the six shuffled along with centimetres between their heads and the top of the tunnel. Even Barney had to scramble on his belly as the gap was too narrow for him to stand.

Daisy inched along in the middle of the group, making slow progress as she edged forward on her forearms and legs. Her thoughts kept darting to what it would be like to get stuck in such a narrow space. Beads of sweat began to appear on her forehead.

"How much longer does this go on for?" she asked, grimacing.

"I can see the end now," said Rufus, holding his torch out with one arm. "It opens up in a bit."

The hole lowered a little and stopped with a drop to the ground.

"Hold my legs," he called behind him.

Maye grabbed Rufus' feet as he reached down to the floor with his hands.

"You can let go now!"

Rufus swung to the floor. Maye catapulted herself to the ground with ease followed down by Lara, Barney, Daisy and Tom.

They turned around to see the remains of living quarters around them. Metal frames of chairs lined the walls and a tin bath that was badly bent out of shape lay to their side. Rufus could not resist jumping inside it.

"Ewww." Lara squirmed. "You're getting covered in muck!"

"Imagine sitting here having a bath, with bombs raining down outside," said Rufus, his eyes wide.

"I'd rather not," said Lara flatly. "Come on, Barney wants us to go that way."

Tom gave Rufus a hand to pull him out of the bath and the small boy wiped the chalk off his jacket and jeans. They followed Barney who was sniffing the ground with keen interest.

After a while they came to another blockage. A wall had been bricked up from the tunnel ceiling to the floor.

"Let's find another way," said Lara. She turned her back to go, but Barney jumped forward onto the brick wall, scratching and barking excitedly.

The others came to take a closer look at the wall.

Tom ran his fingers along a crack. "It's been cut. Right in the middle."

Lara and Tom pushed the area next to the crack and a square section of the wall fell forward with a loud crash.

Barney leapt through the square space in a flash and turned to look at his friends.

"Someone really doesn't want us to go this way," said Rufus, as he climbed through the gap. He turned to look back at the others with a smile. "Guys, this is it!"

Chapter 28
The Final Hiding Place

Once they had all climbed to the other side of the wall, Lara looked over her shoulder.

"Shouldn't we cover the gap?" she asked. "If someone else comes this way they'll know we're here."

With Daisy and Tom, she picked up the square section of brick and replaced it into the slot.

"If this leads to the hiding place... I don't think Frances and Sebastian could've come this way," said Rufus, looking back at the brick wall. "They wouldn't fit through that gap in the clay that we crawled through, since Dee couldn't fit through it either."

"True,' said Lara. "There must be another way in."

They continued along the tunnels until the way forward was obstructed yet again by another wall of clay.

"There's a gap at the top," said Rufus, pointing up. Maye was already climbing up into it.

"Not again," said Daisy, covering her face with her hands. "I hate all these tight spaces!"

Lara smiled at Daisy and put her hand on her friend's shoulder. "It's going to be fine. We're all in this together."

"It's either go through or head back the way we came," said Tom.

"Fine," said Daisy, taking a deep breath. "Let's go!"

Barney leapt up after Maye, and Tom gave Rufus, Daisy and Lara a leg-up before climbing through himself.

The gap was an even tighter squeeze than before, and the ceiling grazed their backs as they wriggled through.

"It's blocked up this end!" yelled Maye.

"What?" yelled Daisy in dismay.

"There's a gap… but it's not big enough to get through."

"Can you make it bigger?" asked Rufus.

Maye pushed with her hands. Some mounds of clay fell to the floor, but not enough to fit her small body through.

"Everyone, go back a bit," she called out. The others shuffled backwards with a series of groans. Even Barney let out a small howl. Maye, with a very limited

165

amount of space, shifted her body round so that she was facing Barney's head. Taking a deep breath, she pulled her legs towards her chest then kicked out as hard and fast as she could. Further clumps of clay fell to the ground. Feeling encouraged, Maye continued until a space widened up that was big enough for her to crawl through and slide herself to the ground.

The rest of the group followed her through. They shone their torches to see a collection of wooden crates against the walls.

Rufus went to one of the containers and pulled back two clasps to open the lid.

"Wow," he gasped, shining his torch inside. A shimmering statue gleamed back at him. "It's gold!"

Lara went over to look. "Is it the stolen Egyptian treasure?"

"I don't think so." Rufus lifted the object from the box. "It's heavy!"

He pulled out a golden statue of a man sitting down, with his hands on his knees.

"It looks Asian," said Lara. "Chinese, maybe."

"This one looks Asian too," said Tom, lifting up a large golden disc with patterns ringed around it.

"Those guys must have stolen so much," said Maye.

Daisy walked around snapping photos on her phone.

"I'm starting a blog," she explained to Maye, who raised an eyebrow.

"Wait… remember when you looked up that article about the robbery?" Lara asked Tom. "Do you still have it on your phone?"

"I've got no signal…" said Tom, staring down at his mobile. "Why?"

"I think the article said there had been some Chinese valuables stolen."

"Yeah, it did," Rufus confirmed. "I remember. It from the house of Lord and Lady… something or other."

"We can't stop and look at it all," said Lara, as Rufus rummaged through more boxes and Daisy snapped more pictures. "There's no chance we can get it all out. We need to see where this passage leads, then get help."

Tom, Maye, Lara and Barney walked forward.

"Rufus, Daisy," called Lara, looking over her shoulder. "Put down the gold! And the phone!"

Rufus and Daisy sighed in unison. Reluctantly, Rufus put down the treasure, and they joined the others.

Around the corner more crates filled the passageway.

"Hold on," said Rufus.

"We *can't* look through any more boxes," said Lara.

"Shhh!" Rufus held his arm out to stop the others. "There's a light coming from around the corner... someone else is here!"

Chapter 29
Trapped

The six were frozen to the spot as they listened, Lara keeping a hand on Barney's collar. Footsteps were coming towards them along with the sound of a woman's voice.

Lara mouthed the word 'Battenbridge' to the others, before pointing to the crates. They all hurried inside them amongst the ancient treasures. For Lara, it was a tight squeeze next to the statue of a dragon with Barney pressed on her lap. She closed the lid right as the Battenbridges turned the corner.

"What time is the truck coming?" asked Frances.

"In about three hours," answered Sebastian. "We'll have the space clear by this afternoon."

"Those awful children," spat Frances venomously. "Meddling in our affairs like this! Once this is over, we'll track them down and make them pay."

The six scarcely dared to breathe in the cramped dark compartments.

"Too right, sister... I say..." Sebastian paused. "This crate's been opened." He flung open the lid and stood back in shock as Rufus jumped out and raced down the corridor. But another man was further down the passageway and grabbed the boy's shoulder.

"Who's this?" said the man, as Rufus wriggled in vain underneath his firm grip.

"It's one of those ghastly children!" shrieked Frances, flinging another crate lid open.

"Come out," called Sebastian. "You're surrounded. If you don't come out now it will be worse for you when we find you."

Lara, fearing for Barney, opened the crate lid and stood up. Tom and Daisy stepped out of their crates.

Frances pointed at Barney. "It's that awful brute, Sebastian!"

"You keep hold of that mutt," warned Sebastian. "Lock them in storage room three."

Four men nudged Lara, Barney, Daisy, Tom and Rufus around the corner where they unbolted a heavy wooden door. They opened it and waved the five inside.

"You can stay there until someone finds you," said one of the men as they bolted the door. "Which could be a very long time!" The men chuckled and the sound of their footsteps faded from earshot.

Rufus, Lara, Daisy and Tom shone their torches onto bare white stone walls.

"They didn't get Maye," whispered Tom, with a hopeful smile. "She'll go back to Dee and Logan and they'll get help."

"They won't be able to come through that way," said Lara, sitting down on the cold floor. "Like Rufus said, the gap in that first rock was too small for Logan and Dee to get through."

"They could get digging equipment or something," said Rufus. "But it could take a while... Sebastian said they had a truck coming in three hours."

"They'll probably tell their driver to come earlier now they know someone could come looking for us," said Daisy, joining Lara on the floor.

Tom paced around the room holding his phone in different spots.

"Still no signal," he said with a sigh.

They all tried hard to think of a way out of their current predicament. Barney started to feel bored and nudged Lara's foot with his nose.

"I haven't got your ball," said Lara. Barney licked her hands and she sighed. "Okay, tricks!"

171

The others watched as Barney followed Lara's commands eagerly.

"Sit... paw... high five... roll... jump... down... play dead..."

"That's it!" cried Rufus. "Play dead!"

"What?" said Tom after a pause.

"At some point they'll send someone in here to check on us... if we all lie on the floor including Barney, we can surprise them and get out of here."

"Ridiculous!" said Lara, frowning. "What if they don't send anyone? Then we're just stuck here pretending to be dead, like a bunch of divs."

"There's nothing else to do though," said Tom, shrugging his shoulders. "I can't pick the lock when it's bolted from the outside."

They waited in silence, with Rufus pressing his ear against the door. After what felt like a year, the sound of voices came towards them.

"Now!" said Rufus, before dramatically flinging himself to the floor.

"Play dead," whispered Lara to Barney.

The heavy door swung open and Bill stood in the doorway beaming out a strong LED torch over four children and a dog, who were all lying face down on the floor. Barney's legs were splayed out by his sides in a most peculiar fashion.

"Stop mucking about," said Bill, his voice a little uncertain. "Give over your mobile phones."

There was no movement from the ground.

"This isn't funny," he said. "'Umphrey, get over 'ere! Something weird's going on with the kids and dog."

Humphrey shuffled in.

"They're pretending," he said.

"Come off it 'Umph! 'Ow's that dog pretending? If 'e was alive 'e'd be biting us."

Humphrey walked in the room and stared down at Barney.

"Bit unnerving, ain't it?" said Bill. "D'ya think there's a poisonous gas in 'ere that's killed 'em all off?"

"Let's check their pulses."

Humphrey stepped over to Lara's motionless body while Bill went over to Rufus. As he flopped the boy's body over, Rufus opened his eyes and let out a blood-curdling scream. Bill and Humphrey jumped back in surprise. Tom, Daisy, Lara and Rufus ran out of the room while Barney barked furiously at the two men, backing them against the wall.

"Barney, come!" called Lara.

The Border collie sprang to Lara's side and she slammed the door shut and bolted it. They fled down the tunnel as Humphrey and Bill pounded the door behind them.

The tunnels were brightened by lights attached to the walls. They ran past a room where two men were packing boxes. They looked up as the four fled past and immediately gave chase.

"Run!" panted Lara.

"We *are* running!" said Rufus.

They raced through the underground corridors, each one gasping for breath, except Barney who would run for hours given the choice.

Tom spotted an open door a few feet away from them. He hoped that there was a lock on the other side. He could hear that the two men were just a few steps behind. Deciding to take a gamble, he skidded to a stop past the door, then slammed it shut behind him. His hands fumbled for a lock. Rufus, Daisy and Lara pushed their weight against the door as the two men barged against it from the other side.

"Hurry!" said Daisy through gritted teeth.

Tom's hands found a bolt at the top of the door and he slid it across.

"Put your hands up and keep hold of that dog."

They turned to see Frances Battenbridge standing in front of them, with both hands clutching a revolver.

Chapter 30
Looking for the Exit

"Up against there," said Frances, tilting the gun towards the wall. The men continued pounding the door.

Tom, Daisy and Rufus backed against the wall, with Lara alongside them holding onto Barney's collar as he growled.

"That *disgusting* brute," sneered Frances, scrunching her face. "I ought to shoot him now and get it over with."

"Don't you dare!" screamed Lara, her face turning red.

"You thought you could outsmart me, didn't you? The Ring has been in place throughout London for decades, funnelling goods across London and out of the country through Dover. And we'll keep going long after you have all been… extinguished."

"The police will catch up with you," said Rufus.

Frances threw her head back and laughed.

"You simpleton! My family would be the last people the police would suspect. The Battenbridges are pillars of society."

Tom spotted a torch attached to the wall past Frances' head. He carefully searched the wall with his hands hidden behind his back.

"Pillars of society?" said Lara, frowning. "You're nothing but a pair of dirty crooks."

"We are not *crooks*! We bring the finest antiquities of the world to the finest families who can afford to pay for them. Otherwise, treasures like these would be languishing in rotten museums and universities just to be studied by nasty little students and failing academics like your mother! Yes, I saw her at the awards luncheon. Sarah Jacobs spends all her time trying to bring knowledge to the lowlife masses, when only a select few can truly appreciate what these treasures are worth."

"You're not only a crook," said Daisy, pointing, "you're a snob!"

Frances' face erupted in anger as her indignation boiled over. She cocked the gun and at that moment Tom ripped one of the torches from the wall behind him and flung it straight towards the woman's wrist. Frances shrieked as the gun fell towards Rufus' feet. He kicked it away. Frances made a dash for it, but Daisy stuck out a foot and she crashed to the floor.

Lara moved forward with Barney. "Stay down there or I'll set my dog on you!"

Tom took a rope from his rucksack and quickly tied Frances' hands and feet together behind her back, whilst she launched a barrage of threats.

"Quick, let's go!" said Rufus. They ran away down the corridor leaving Frances wriggling on the floor in fury.

The five fled down through the tunnels, passing more and more boxes of treasures. They all longed for daylight and fresh air. Finally, they saw a light ahead of them coming from the sky.

"It's the way out," said Lara breathlessly. "We made it!"

A tall figure came running towards them from the other side of their escape route.

"It's Sebastian!" said Tom, his face falling. "He's going to get to the hatch before us!"

"Out of my way!" came a voice behind them.

Lara, Tom, Daisy and Barney jumped into an alcove as Rufus came charging past them with an extremely rusty shopping trolley containing a heavy box.

"Arrrrrrrrrrrrrrrrrrrrrrrr!" he yelled, accelerating down the sloping tunnel. He raised his fist in the air as he hopped onto the back of the bolting trolley. "Charrrrrge!"

Sebastian looked up in shock as the trolley pounded him in the chest. He held on tight to the front of the trolley until it crashed into a wall.

Rufus jumped off the back of the trolley and dashed towards the escape hatch. Tom, Daisy and Lara had already lifted Barney up into the open air and hauled themselves up. Tom and Lara grabbed Rufus' hands and pulled him out.

"I think I... winded him..." said Rufus as he gasped for breath. "But he'll be back!"

The five were inside a large field in the freezing December air. Tom, Daisy and Lara lifted a metal hatch back over the hole.

"There's a lock, but no key," said Daisy.

"I'll try and hold it shut," said Tom. "We need something to weigh it down."

Daisy pressed down on the metal with Tom, while Rufus and Lara ran to look for any heavy objects. They picked up a rock between them and lugged it back to the hatch.

"I don't think it's enough," said Tom, as they dumped it down. "I've got a signal now, I'll call Logan."

Lara pointed to the sky. "No need…"

A helicopter zoomed over the landscape towards them. They waved their arms as it got closer. Inside, hovering above ground, were Dee, Logan and Maye.

Chapter 31
The End of the Adventure

The helicopter lowered to the ground, sending gusts of wind across the fields. Barney circled the aircraft in excitement, leaping and barking, while Rufus, Lara, Daisy and Tom desperately tried to hold onto the hatch door as Sebastian hammered against it from underground.

Logan jumped out before the helicopter had come to a complete stop.

"Are you alright?" he yelled over the deafening sound of the blades.

"We need something heavy to weigh this down," said Lara. "Sebastian's under here!"

Logan ran to the side of the field and staggered back with a huge boulder. The others sprang out of the way as he dumped it onto the trapdoor with a yell of relief.

Dee had landed the helicopter and was walking over with Maye.

Rufus ran over and high-fived them both. "How did you know we'd be here? We didn't even know we'd be here!"

"It's all thanks to Maye," said Dee, smiling.

"When you got captured, I went back the way we came. Logan and Dee were too big to get through, so they told the security and they went to get some digging equipment to make a bigger hole."

"In the meantime, we knew the gang must have got in from another entrance," continued Dee, "so, I called a friend who knows someone at the local airfield so we could borrow a chopper and look for an opening above ground."

"We'd only been in the air about ten minutes before we saw you waving," said Logan.

"Come on!" Maye skipped over to the others and waved them over with her hands. "Let's go to the cops so they can get the bad guys."

With everyone on-board, Dee piloted the helicopter back into the air. They zipped over fields towards the white chalk cliffs.

"Everything's all *white*," said Maye as she stroked Barney's fur.

"Alright?" yelled Rufus over the din of the chopper. "I can't hear you!"

"No!" shouted Maye. "All white. Look!"

Flakes of snow floated around them and drifted over the cliffs and waves.

"Told you it would snow," beamed Maye.

***

Mr Rottin strode through the corridors of Swindlebrook Secondary School, glaring at the students as he made his way towards detention. He hated the first few weeks of a new term almost as much as he hated supervising detention. The two combined were a perfect storm of misery. He spotted a sandy head amongst the year sevens.

"Kexley," his voice boomed.

Rufus turned around. "Mr Rotten?"

Mr Rottin glanced down at his list of detention attendees absently, not registering Rufus' mispronunciation of his name.

"You've not been on detention yet this year," he said, a note of surprise in his voice. "You heeded my advice, I see. Hopefully, you're not using your freedom to cause havoc outside school to make up for your lack of exploits inside school."

"Freedom? I'm grounded for a month."

"Aha!" Mr Rottin folded his arms and lifted his nose into the air. "I knew you'd been up to something! What did you do?"

"Chased a gang of criminals across London with my cousin, her dog, Daisy and my mate Tom, without telling Auntie Sarah about it."

"There's no need to make up stories, Kexley."

"It's not! It was in the papers and everything!"

"What was?"

"The Battenbridge family and their stolen goods."

Mr Rottin's mouth opened in surprise.

"That was all over the papers," he said. "They got caught in Dover. When the police found them there was a load of treasure underground and a computer chip that had a database of the location of every piece of treasure that the family had ever sold, dating back to just after World War Two. And their next target was going to be the Crown Jewels…"

"I know," said Rufus. "I was there."

"The news did mention about some kids and a dog that somehow got caught up in all that… that was you?"

"Yeah."

"So, you helped find decades' worth of stolen valuables… and your aunt still grounded you for a month?"

"It was going to be two months, but we got a month knocked off for discovering millions of pounds worth of treasure."

At that moment, Lara was walking down the corridor linking arms with Daisy.

"Ah, Lara," said Mr Rottin. "You're a sensible, honest girl. Your cousin has just told me the most fantastical story about your Christmas holidays…"

"Hey!" interrupted Rufus.

"I know, right," said Lara. "Sometimes the truth is stranger than fiction. Come on, Rufus, there's a reporter that wants to Skype us tonight about the treasure we found. Mum said if we're late for school pick-up she'll increase our grounding by a week."

"Seeya, Mr Rottin!" said Daisy with a grin.

Rufus, Daisy and Lara went out of the school's main doors into the car park, leaving Mr Rottin gaping after them in astonishment.

Acknowledgements

As I write these acknowledgements in early 2020, it is almost exactly a year since the first book in The Adventurers Series was published. I have so many people to thank for all the support they have shared with me during my own publishing adventures.

Thank you to my mum Dawn for all your kindness and for pushing my books onto anyone who shows the slightest bit of interest! Thank you to my brother Jeff for providing the inspiration for the bus in this story.

Thank you to all my friends – there are so many of you right back from pre-school days to school, university and various jobs who have shown so much enthusiasm for my writing. Thank you to the children who attended writing workshops with me this year – keep writing, I want to be reading your books in a few years' time!

A big shout out to the team of professionals who helped turn this story into a book – to Andrew Smith for your amazing cover art, Amanda Horan at Let's Get Booked for your skilful editing and Helen Baggott for proofreading.

As always, my biggest thank you is to you, reader! Thank you for continuing with The Adventurers and with me. I hope you enjoy these stories as much as I enjoy creating them.

About the Author

Jemma Hatt grew up near Sevenoaks in Kent where she developed a passion for reading and writing short stories, which ultimately led to a degree in English Literature from the University of Exeter.

The Adventurers Series was inspired by many family holidays to Devon and Cornwall, as well as the adventure stories she loved reading as a child. After having lived and worked in London, New York and Delaware, Jemma is now based in Kent and working on the next Adventurers stories as well as other writing projects.

Stay up-to-date with Jemma's writing, and access free giveaways and offers by signing up to her newsletter at www.jemmahatt.com (if you are under 13 please ask an adult to sign up for you).

THE ADVENTURERS AND THE CONTINENTAL CHASE

By Jemma Hatt

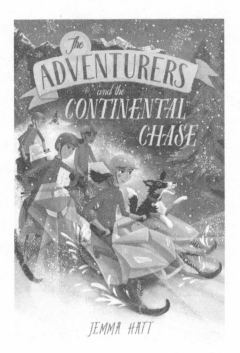

A kidnap in Paris… a chase across Europe… one epic road trip!

The Adventurers are on holiday when Maye warns of suspicious activity in Paris. Join them as they race from the French Alps to the ancient ruins of Rome on the trail of a dangerous gang with a legacy of secrets.